To Oz and Back

To Oz and Back

Alexandra Eden

a Bones & the Duchess Mystery

ALLEN A. KNOLL, PUBLISHERS

SANTA BARBARA, CA

Allen A. Knoll, Publishers, 200 West Victoria Street,
Santa Barbara, CA 93101
(805) 564-3377
bookinfo@knollpublishers.com

First Edition

06 05 04 03   5 4 3 2 1

Library of Congress Cataloging-in-Publication Data

Eden, Alexandra.
  To Oz and back : a Bones and the Duchess mystery / Alexandra Eden.--1st ed.
      p. cm.
  Summary: Bones, a former police officer, teams up with Verity, a clever
twelve-year-old with Asperger's syndrome, to try to solve the mystery of two missing
girls.
      ISBN 1-888310-22-7 (alk. paper)
   [1. Missing children--Fiction. 2. Asperger's syndrome--Fiction. 3.
Cryptography--Fiction. 4. Mystery and detective stories.] I. Title.

PZ7.E22 to 2002
[Fic]--dc21   2002034100

Printed by Sheridan Books in Chelsea, MI
text typeface is Goudy 13 point
Smyth sewn case bind with Skivertex Series 1 cloth

One

The duchess made her appearance at the Broad Street Hotel as she always did—with that regal way she had of walking. No running and jumping, hopping and skipping like other girls her age—she did that I might have called her a princess. That was one of the things that made you like her—she wasn't hung up on being like everybody else.

"Hi, Duchess," I said from my rocking chair on the front porch. She didn't take her backpack off to sit, so she was on the edge of the rocker like a grasshopper on too small a leaf. I'd seen her come down the sidewalk all serious-like. I always said 'hello' first. Like she was shy, but she really wasn't—just sort of in her own world. "What's new?" I asked.

She sat in the rocker next to mine. She didn't look at me when she spoke but stared straight ahead, as though there was something fascinating going on at the corner grocery store. But while she was staring across the street, she answered my question.

"Wanda didn't come to school today."

"Oh?" I said, not that I knew who Wanda was. Not that I cared. But I am a social guy. "Flu?" I asked. It was going around.

"No," she said, as though I were the biggest

dummy on the block. "She disappeared."

"Disappeared?" Now I was interested. "How do you know?"

"Her mother said so."

"You talk to her mother, do you?"

"She called me to ask if I knew anything."

"Do you?" I asked.

"No. But maybe I can figure it out—"

"*You?*"

"Yes—I am going to try to help find her."

Now, I don't mean to be rude or a wet blanket or anything, but I didn't see how the duchess had any hope of bringing that off. Me, being an ex-policeman, I can see finding a missing girl. But I didn't say anything. Not wanting to discourage the hopes of a twelve year old.

The duchess was a cute kid with chocolate brown hair that hit her shoulders. She was about a foot shorter than I was. Her eyes were black as coals and when she looked straight at you, you couldn't tell what she was thinking. She had full lips and a cute little nose. And the nicest way about her. Like a young duchess.

"What did her mother say?"

"Wanda kissed her goodbye this morning; she told her mother she loved her. She left the house to catch the school bus, but she didn't get to it. No one in the neighborhood saw her anywhere this morning."

"What neighborhood is she from?"

"Country Club Circle."

That was the richest part of town. Big houses on the Country Club golf course.

"Any ransom note?" I asked.

She shook her head. "Mrs. Trexler called the school, and the principal asked the class if anyone knew anything."

"Did they?"

"No one said they did."

"You think maybe someone knew something?"

"I don't know," she said, but the cagey way she said it made me wonder if she suspected something.

"What's her family like?"

"Her dad's a doctor."

"What does Mom do? She work, keep house, or what?"

"She stays at home."

"You ever been to their house?"

She nodded. "We're in the Girl Scouts together. Mrs. Trexler is our leader."

"Who are Wanda's friends?"

"Her best friend is Arvilla Easterbrook. She lives down the street from her."

"She in the Girl Scouts too?"

"Yes."

That was one of the things about the duchess—she didn't say yeah or use any sloppy speech like other kids her age. Always correct and formal English. Delivered in her flat voice. That's because she has Asperger's.

I want to say right up front, I solved the case, not the little girl. I was a policeman after all, and I know what I am doing. I don't mean she didn't help out here and there, but anybody who says the duchess solved it is giving her too much credit. They think that just because I was invited to leave the force for the dumbest reason doesn't mean I'm incompetent. Firing Bones Fatzinger like that was overdoing it.

Some name, huh? I was christened James Allen Fatzinger, but when I was a kid I was pretty skinny and my bones stuck out. So they called me Bones, and it stuck. I'm a little on the heavy side now, so some think it's sort of a joke calling me Bones, but trying to get anyone to call me Jim now is a losing battle.

I still have my hair color—blonde, sort of, like most of the Pennsylvania Germans around here. We call them Pennsylvania Dutch, but that's from Deutsch, the German word for German. I have all my teeth and my skin isn't so bad except for the red around my eyes that comes when I'm excited and goes when I'm not.

I stand about five foot eight, and I wasn't a very threatening cop. That was part of my problem.

I've had a few girlfriends in my time, but nothing took. Women are attracted to uniforms, they tell me, and since I'm off the force I haven't been attracting any. I'm not too old to think of marriage. It all just seems like a lot of effort.

I befriended the duchess out of human kindness. She doesn't have friends. That's a symptom of Asperger's Syndrome, which is sort of an autism "lite."

People with Asperger's can be very intelligent, as Verity is. Their speech is something of a drone without the inflections. They can fixate on certain things to the exclusion of others and have a fantastic memory. Verity is the state spelling champ for her age.

I'm told these things that make up Asperger's

can vary in individuals—some fixate more than others, some have better memories, and so forth.

I wouldn't know—I've never known anyone besides Verity who had it.

We have a lot more diseases now than when I was a kid. I've tried to account for it, but I can't. Is it television, computers, game boy, pesticides, preservatives in food, drugs or all the new medicines? Carbon monoxide from all the cars? I don't know if that's what did it to the duchess or not.

In my day we had a kid or two in school who was slow, but we didn't have any fancy names for them. The duchess isn't slow by any means, just so we understand she's not any smarter than I am—no way could she have solved such a tough case. I mean, if the FBI couldn't crack it, how would you expect a twelve year old to?

I was getting interested in the case. Once you have police work in your blood you can't get it out. I wondered what my old friends in the department were doing about the case. Maybe I'd wander over there—I'd check on the real story. I didn't expect the duchess to know as much as she was making believe. Kids make things up.

Suddenly the duchess stood up, shifted her backpack (which was loaded with books) and went into the hotel.

Two

The duchess's name is really Verity Buscador, but I call her the duchess because she acts like royalty and looks like she's full of wisdom. Don't get me wrong—I don't think she knows everything, she just *looks* that way.

How I met the duchess is I live at the Broad Street Hotel in Ephesus, PA. The proprietors, Clint and Clara Rudy, are Verity's grandparents—and she comes to visit every day. I remember her as a little kid, afraid to cross the street. Now she's a duchess.

Some would say it's odd for an older man like myself to befriend a twelve year-old girl—but after I left the force, my days were not full by any stretch of the imagination. And this little kid was underfoot and lonely, so I just took to passing the time of day with her, and so when I got on the kidnapping case, it was natural to schmooze with her about it—like I could get some insight into the minds of girls her age.

Being an ex-cop I had my theories, and being a resident of the Broad Street Hotel—taking all my meals there, hanging out in the soda fountain Clint had set up across the hall from the dining room—I naturally talked to people who were very interested in my ideas about the case. People want answers to these mysteries, and in this case, there were no easy answers.

The Broad Street Hotel was on Broad Street—surprise, surprise. On one side was an auto repair garage—just a garage where Jacob repaired cars. It was part of the hotel property, so I expect old Clint was collecting some rent from him.

Behind the hotel on the side street was a mortuary—the Ritter Funeral Home.

The hotel was a long, flat two and a half story building with a turret on the corner to make it look deluxe. The third floor was under a slanting roof with dormer windows, poking out of the roof like they do. The front porch ran the whole length of the building like one of those seashore hotels where everyone could sit out on hot nights and enjoy the salt air.

The view was of the corner store across the street and some double houses. If they hadn't been in the way you might have seen the South Street Mountain from the porch.

I sat out there myself many times watching the world go by. Not that much of the world went by on Broad Street—it was one street up from the main Street and sort of out of the way.

The thing about Broad street was that it wasn't what you'd call broad today—but back in the horse and buggy days when it was built it seemed pretty broad.

I know Clint was happy to have me as a boarder at the hotel—even if I was sometimes a little behind on my rent. When you have a business establishment like the Broad Street, you can do a lot worse than have an ex-officer of the law settin' on the front porch, keeping an eye on things. I never asked Clint or Clara for a penny for watching the place, and I just know he had to appreciate it.

So I was off to my old stomping grounds—the police station. It was just around the corner from the hotel.

The station was really three rooms in the borough hall which was built out of bricks. I always thought of the three little pigs when I looked at it. It was three stories and one of the biggest buildings in town. The volunteer fire company had its trucks next to the police offices. We had three cops, and my replacement was a kid wet behind the ears named Milton Urfer. We called him Milt.

The cop on duty when I got there was Pete Peters—Grumbera was his nickname. Pennsylvania Dutch for potatoes—he ate a lot of them. But it wasn't the potatoes that done him in, it was all the butter he put on them. Maybe butterball would have been a better name. Good thing we didn't have a lot of crime in town—I can't see him jumping any fences in a chase.

Being so small a town, with pretty heavy Dutchmen, we tend to overlook excess weight. Now if I were still on the force, I'd be fit and trim.

"How's it going, Grumbera?" I asked. He was sitting behind his desk looking for a window to stare out of. There were none. The main room had a distant window—we used to joke no windows was somebody's idea of safety for the troops.

"Not too bad," Grumbera said. "Yourself?"

"Peaches and cream," I said. I had a way of talking that was colorful when I wanted it to be. "Hear the Trexler girl is missing."

"Yup. Went for the school bus this morning and never got it."

"Theories?"

"They're out combing the park by the river now," he said, shaking his head. "Not good."

"Suspects?"

"Nothing yet. Mother is pretty upset."

"Imagine," I said.

"School called her to ask where Wanda was. They do that when they don't have any excuse from the parent. Good thing too—they started looking right away. Mother was a Girl Scout leader, she called all the girls. Nothing."

"Ransom note?"

"Nothing yet."

We chewed the fat a while longer, but I was surprised he didn't seem to know any more than the duchess.

"Well, Grumbera, if you need another hand—sweeping the park, whatever, I'm available."

He looked uncomfortable at the offer. He shifted his potato body in his chair. "Much obliged, Bones," he said. "You know the folks are still nervous about you."

"No reason," I said.

"Well," Grumbera frowned, "people around here get funny ideas once you get canned. It's no secret the chief thought you were too soft to be a policeman."

"Being nice to people isn't soft—it's nice."

"Yeah, well, cops are supposed to be tough."

"In a small town like this? Life is tough enough without us adding to it."

"We're in the business of putting the bad guys in jail. That's what the bosses want. You answer a call at the grocery store—guy holding them up to steal food—and you don't arrest him—you pay for the food and let him go."

"His family was starving."

"You ought to be a social worker," Grumbera said.

"That's what the chief said," I remembered aloud.

"Yeah, and it didn't help when you bad-mouthed the chief and the mayor and the mayor over-heard you."

I shrugged my shoulders. "How could I know?"

"I guess—but that's just it. You weren't careful."

"You do the right thing you don't have to be so careful."

"Letting hold-up men go is not the right thing if you're a cop."

"Hold up? He had ten bucks worth of stuff and told 'em he'd pay next week."

"Did the owner agree to that?"

"Well, no—"

"So he walked out with the stuff."

"I guess."

"Down here we call that robbery. You can't just go around making nice for everybody. It's not police work."

"Well maybe it should be."

"You'll never change, Bones."

"Thank you."

"It wasn't a compliment."

"Not to you maybe. To me it was high praise." I smiled. He didn't smile back. "Well, maybe I can develop something on my own. Truth to tell, I'm not that busy at present."

"You want to be careful, Bones," he said. "Sticking your nose in where it's not wanted, you could get it cut off."

"Oh, yeah," I said. "I'm careful all right, real careful."

I left his tiny office and decided to check on the action down by the river. It wasn't more than a couple of miles, and the fresh air would do me good. It was a free country after all, and nobody could keep me from taking a walk if I wanted to.

Three

There wasn't much action at the river. Everyone had pretty much left. There was one volunteer policeman still there, and he told me they hadn't found anything.

I hiked back up the hill to the hotel. I had my dinner and went to bed. I couldn't sleep for wondering about the missing girl.

The next afternoon I sat in the hotel dining room with all the painted murals of cow pastures and barnyards on the walls and read my newspaper.

Clara, the cook and owner's wife, was at another table making her shopping list. It was Wednesday, that meant sauerkraut and pork for dinner. Tomorrow would be chicken pot pie, my favorite. Last night we had pot roast. Made things simpler for the cook to follow the same menu every week.

"Clara," I said, "is Verity stopping in after school today?"

"Always does," she said, not looking up from her list. "Why? You need her?"

"Of course I don't need her. I was just curious. I'm onto this missing girl case," I explained, perhaps exaggerating just a bit. "She knows the girl's mother. I'd like her to arrange for me to talk to Mrs. Trexler."

"You're on the case?" Now she looked up, and I could see in her face she didn't believe me. "I thought you…left…the police department."

"Privately," I said. I kept my voice down—I didn't want to brag.

"Then I suppose we can look for some of the back rent you owe?" The way she said it, it didn't seem like she believed it.

"Well, I, ah, I haven't actually been promised any money…yet—that's one of the things I need to talk to Mrs. Trexler about."

"Uh huh," she nodded, as though she were reading my mind. That was the thing about Clara, you always got the feeling she saw right inside you—and *through* you. Clara was the one always needling me for the rent—Clint couldn't have cared less. He knew what my presence around there was worth.

I figured I spent so little time in my room on the second floor, I shouldn't have to pay so much.

Not that my room wasn't nice or anything, but it was small—and kind of dark. There was a bed—a narrow twin, a desk, a straight back chair and one easy chair. Oh, and there was a table by the bed with a lamp on it for reading. The window had a shade you pulled down at night. The maid cleaned and changed the sheets once a week.

The paper had quite a spread about the missing Trexler girl and how it had scared the living daylights out of the people in town. Everybody was waiting for the ransom note, the Trexlers being probably the richest family in town.

There was a picture of Wanda in the paper. She

13

looked like a happy enough kid—but that was hard to tell from a snapshot—someone had probably said, "Smile—say cheese—" and she had. Anyway, she was a towhead with curly locks falling to her shoulders.

I tried to picture Wanda and Verity, the duchess, in Girl Scouts together, and wondered how they interacted. Asperger's kids were not supposed to be big on making friends, so maybe they weren't close. I always had trouble making friends whenever I went any place new, so I got to wondering what it would be like if you didn't want to make friends—or didn't *need* to. It might be a relief. So maybe this Asperger's wasn't that bad after all.

The paper gave a hotline telephone number to call if anyone had seen Wanda Trexler.

The duchess came in, her backpack stuffed with books. It was like the backpack wanted to pull her back, but she leaned forward to neutralize the pull.

"Hi, Duchess—"

"Hello."

"Come sit here a minute," I said. She looked at Clara as if for approval.

"Cookies are in the kitchen," Clara said, and Verity threw off her book backpack, dropped it on the table and made a b-line for the kitchen. She returned with a plate of chocolate chip cookies and plumped down next to me, setting the plate in front of her. She was already eating one of them. She didn't offer me any.

"Duchess," I said, "you think you could arrange a meeting with me for Wanda's mother?"

"What for?"

"I want to help her find Wanda."

She chewed on that and the cookie for a while. "I guess so," she said.

"When, do you think?"

"Right now, if you want."

"Now? Do you think that would be all right with her?"

"You can call her and ask."

"Me? How about *you* call her? I don't know her—" or anybody else in her social class, I thought to myself.

"Okay," she said, taking another cookie with her to the phone in the kitchen. I heard her dial—she had the number memorized. She had a good head for numbers—"Hello, Mrs. Trexler," she said politely. "This is Verity. There's this man who used to be a policeman here—Bones Fatzinger—" she tittered—no doubt at my name. "He wants to talk to you to see if he can help find Wanda." Verity paused to listen, then said. "Okay, we'll be right out."

"Come on," she said, picking up the last cookie.

"Now?" I said. "You got her to agree to see me now?"

"Us," she corrected me. "I have to go along."

"Well, geez, Verity, I mean, couldn't you bow out for some reason? This is grown-up stuff."

"Yes, and the grown up called Mrs. Trexler on the telephone."

Sometimes she got off zingers like that.

Four

I used to drive out to Country Club Circle, just to see how rich people lived. I'd drive down the street and imagine I was in a new Cadillac or something and try to feel what it was like to live in this ritzy neighborhood. I couldn't imagine it. Some of the houses were almost as big as the Broad Street Hotel.

The duchess and I walked out to Country Club Circle. Her house was on the way and she dropped off her backpack. I waited for her on the sidewalk. Her mother was a lawyer who worked at home, and I didn't want to bother her.

I was brainstorming with the duchess. "Duchess, I have to prepare for when we get the ransom note. That's where it takes experience. It's a psychological game with a kidnapper. You have to psyche them out. Can't be afraid."

She said, "There might not be a ransom note."

"I'm afraid, Duchess," I said, "you are only showing your inexperience and immaturity. The daughter of one of the town's most prominent—and *wealthy* families disappears and no one wants money for her return? No, I'm afraid this is a clear cut kidnapping, and it's only a matter of time till we get a ransom note."

"Maybe," she said, "maybe not."

My mother told me never to argue with children, it was a hopeless undertaking—so I held my tongue.

The Trexler house was made of gray stone and it rambled all over the place. The back of it faced the Country Club golf course. I never knew what was so wonderful about living in a place where golfers walked by your backyard all the time. I guess you could look out on a lot of grass you didn't have to mow.

When we got to the door, I rang the bell. Mrs. Trexler answered the door herself. I don't know why I expected a maid or a butler. She gave us a reserved smile and said, "Hello, Verity—" then she looked at me. "You must be Mr. Fatzinger." I allowed as how I was and she said, "I'm Elsie Trexler, come in." And we did.

I always took it as a measure of the person how they handled my name. Did they smirk when they said it, or did they just pronounce it as though they were saying Smith or Laudenslager? Elsie handled it okay.

She was a good-looking woman somewhere in her forties. Medium height, just the right size for the expensive clothes she wore. Her hair was blond and pulled back in a bun, as though the seriousness of the event required a serious hairdo. She was probably a little heavier than when she was married, but not too much. In the Pennsylvania Dutch country, she was considered thin. Her red eyes made her look like she had been doing some heavy crying.

"Want to sit down?" she said when we were

inside her warm and expensive living room. I watched to see where she wanted to sit. It was a big old-fashioned armchair covered in some fabric with big old-fashioned pink roses on it.

I sat facing her on a couch with pink and blue stripes. The duchess sat beside me. I was not comfortable interviewing this woman about a crime that could become very emotional with a kid beside me, but Verity was apparently part of the package.

"I'm sorry about Wanda," I began.

Mrs. Trexler closed her eyes and nodded. "It's the most terrible thing that's ever happened to us," she said.

"Any ransom demands yet?"

"Not yet—I'm sitting by the phone. My husband is by the phone in his office. We're on pins and needles."

"Have either of you made any enemies?"

"Wanda? Or my husband?"

"Anyone you can think of?"

"No—and I've tried. Oh, I know there are people who don't like us. Resent us for our standard of living. Our money."

"Any unhappy patients of your husband's…"

"Not that we can think of. He's had no malpractice suits—no—it's just crazy. Here one day we have a nice, quiet, loving family, and then—" she closed her eyes and shook her head again, "—this happens."

"Why do bad things have to happen to good people?" I said, shaking my head along with Mrs. Trexler. "I want to help you find her."

"I appreciate that," she said. She didn't mention money and I didn't have the heart to bring it up. "The police, the FBI, everybody is working. Did you have any kidnappings while you were a...policeman?" She said it in the way you talk about delicate topics. She was sensitive to my position or lack of one and I appreciated that.

"Not in Ephesus," I said, leaving the impression I might have worked elsewhere on kidnapping.

"It just doesn't make sense," she said. "Not unless it's money—Wanda's so *young*, and she'd *never* run away from home—she's just not like that. Why, she has *everything* here. But why don't they send a ransom note so we know she's all right? This is sheer torture to keep us in the dark like this."

She looked at Verity. "She never said anything to you about running away, did she?"

"No, ma'am."

"You don't think she did, do you?"

"No ma'am," the duchess said, aiming to please.

Well, I thought, if she was trying to convince herself that Wanda was taken by someone who wasn't going to hurt her, I thought she should allow the possibility of Wanda's running away. But I guess that would make the parents look bad.

"What was the last thing you remember?" I asked. "Before Wanda left the house?"

"She said, 'So long, Mom—I love you.'"

"Are you sure?"

"Yes, I'm sure—" Mrs. Trexler didn't like the question.

"Yes, of course. I just thought—well, do twelve year olds tell their mothers they love them? Isn't that unusual?"

"I don't know about other twelve year olds—but...well, I guess...she doesn't say it...that...often."

"Think she knew she was going to disappear?"

"Run away? Wanda? Never."

"Ever argue or anything?"

"Argue? Sure. What mother doesn't argue with her twelve year old?"

"Anything unusual?"

"Unusual?"

"A big—bad argument. Major disagreement?"

She was considering something, but shook her head.

We heard some noise outside. It was a car in the garage and Mrs. Trexler jumped up, twisting her hands. "It's my husband," she said, and I couldn't tell if that news made her happy or scared. But it stopped her talking and we all stood around waiting for his entrance like we were expecting the King of England or something.

When he came in, I could see why. He was a tall, impressive man, with a perfect blue suit and red and blue striped tie, and he moved easily to give his wife a kiss. I wondered if he did that when he didn't have an audience.

"Dear," Mrs. Trexler said, "this is Bones Fatzinger—he wants to help find Wanda, and you know Verity. Bones, this is Dr. Trexler."

I nodded, he seemed to consider if my hand—now stretched out toward him—was worth shaking.

But finally he took it, and said modestly, "Hank Trexler. It's good of you to be interested. We need all the help we can get—but I think the police, state police and FBI are doing all that can be done."

"I'm sure," I said. "Sometimes it doesn't hurt to have a fresh eye—someone who isn't connected to or beholden to any organization."

"Be that as it may, I think we're in good hands with *regular* policemen." I caught the slam at me for not being on the force any longer, but what could I say? He nodded at his wife. "We'll talk it over and let you know if you can do something." The way he said "do something" made me think the something he had in mind was taking out the garbage.

I nodded. "Thanks," I said.

The duchess and I said goodbye to them and the last thing we heard was the master's voice saying, "Elsie, where's my drink?"

"Want to talk to Arvilla?" the duchess asked me as we walked down the Trexler's path to the sidewalk.

"Who?"

"Arvilla, Wanda's best friend."

"Oh, yeah—sure. She live around here?"

"Down the street," she said. "Come, I'll take you."

"We don't have to call first?"

"No. The Easterbrooks are not as formal as the Trexlers."

I'm not saying the duchess was no help at all. All I'm saying is giving her credit for solving the case is a big exaggeration.

Five

The Easterbrook house was low and flat, long and modern. Squarish. Lot of glass for this neck of the woods because it gets so cold in the winter. The front yard was not as neat as the Trexlers down the street, and I thought the house needed painting. The Easterbrook house was across the street from the golf course lots.

There was some broken concrete on the path to the door. "The doorbell doesn't work," the duchess said, so I knocked. There was loud music coming from within—the kind of boom-boom-boom sounds the duchess's generation *calls* music. To me it's just noise. Really *loud* noise.

In a minute we realized no one could hear the knock with that racket going on inside. I knocked again—louder.

In a few moments a little urchin opened the door. She was so small it was hard to believe she was the same age as the duchess.

"Oh hi, Verity," the little kid said, proving she was old enough to talk. "Come on in." She didn't ask who I was or even look at me.

We went through the living room and kitchen to what was laughingly called a family room—but there was so much junk in it, no family I ever knew was small enough to fit. The family room was the source of the banging music and Arvilla must have wanted us to get as close as possible to the speakers.

"Arvilla, this is Bones Fatzinger. He used to be a policeman."

"Oh," she said, looking at me for the first time. "Yeah, I heard."

I didn't like that, but you couldn't live in a town this size and not have everybody know your business.

"Bummer about Wanda, huh?" Arvilla said, and it was hard for me to tell what she meant. Was she really sad—or bummed as she would say—or was she indifferent?

"When did you see her last?" I asked.

"I don't know. After school the day before yesterday, I guess."

"Anything seem unusual?"

"Nah."

"Did you see Wanda going for the bus?"

"Nah. I don't know what happened because she didn't make it to the bus."

I turned to the duchess—"You don't ride the bus? How come?"

"I'm closer, and I like to walk."

"Say, Arvilla," I said, "is your mother home?"

"Nah—she's shopping. She *loves* to shop."

"What does she like to shop for?"

"Dresses, clothes, and stuff. Shoes. She has a lot of shoes," she said, rolling her eyes.

"Your dad okay with that? All the shopping?"

"I guess he wasn't. So he left."

"Left?" But as I asked it, I realized I'd heard that.

"Yeah. 'Went south,' my mom says."

"How long ago?"

"Years," she said wearily, like nothing bored her more than talking about this. "I was about five."

"Do you see him?"

"Nah—"

"Do you want to?"

She shrugged. "I don't think *he* wants to," she said sadly.

"Miss him?"

"I don't remember him all that much."

"What do you think happened to Wanda?"

"Don't know," she said.

"Was she happy at home?"

"Yeah, I guess. *I* wouldn't be happy in that place, but it didn't bother Wanda."

"Could she have run away from home?"

She shook her head. "I'd have known about it."

"So was she kidnapped?"

Arvilla shrugged her shoulders. "I guess."

"Scary, isn't it?"

"Yeah, I guess."

I noticed the duchess was staring intently at her friend, Arvilla, as though she were memorizing every word and movement of her face.

"But your mother left you alone in the house. I don't believe the door was even locked, was it?"

"Nah, we don't lock our doors. Mom says someone wants to get in they'll break the door down—or the windows, so why have broken windows on top of everything else?"

"But isn't she worried that what happened to your best friend might happen to you?"

"Nah, she says who'd want me? We aren't rich enough to pay anyone to get me back—not like the Trexler's. Besides, she says I'm so ornery if anyone *did* take me they'd bring me back after five minutes."

Well, I thought, someone has a sense of humor.

I watched the girls. They didn't seem to interact. Arvilla was fiddling with a world class collection of teddy bears and Verity stood off to the side watching. Studying would be more like it. Arvilla didn't offer Verity a teddy bear and Verity didn't ask to participate.

There was a screeching of brakes and commotion outside. I looked at Verity, and she looked at me.

"Mom's home," Arvilla said.

Before I saw her, I heard footsteps.

When she came into the room with her arms full of silver and gold wrapped packages, all I saw of her was her head peeking through the bundles. She had stringy black hair that was not kept any neater than her daughter's and rather large, thick glasses in purple frames that swooped up at the corners to make her look like an owl.

"Oh, Arvilla!" the mom said all excited, "I got the greatest stuff. Wait till you see."

She found a place to dump the packages—I don't know how she did that.

"Oh geez, Arvilla, I missed my shrink appointment I got so carried away at the store."

She continued to converse with Arvilla as though Verity and I were nowhere in sight. Arvilla picked up on it before her mother did. "*Mom!*" she said. "Do you know Bones Fatzinger?"

"Oh," she said, noticing me for the first time. "I saw Verity and I guess I didn't think, I just assumed it was your father, Verity, dear. Can you *ever* forgive me?"

Verity didn't answer. I don't think an answer was expected. I don't know how Verity liked being talked to like that, I don't think much—but you couldn't always tell what she was thinking by the look on her face, it was always more or less the same—kind of blank. I thought that might be a nice advantage in a poker game, but I didn't think the duchess played poker.

"Bones is asking about Wanda."

"Wanda?" This woman was out of it.

"You know," Arvilla insisted—"the kidnapping or whatever."

"Oh, of course, I don't know what I could have been thinking. A *terrible* thing, and right on this block."

"Any theories?"

"Not me," she said. "Floored me like everyone else, I guess."

"You know the girl at all? Wanda?"

"Wanda? Of course, she was Arvilla's best friend."

"What kind of kid is Wanda?"

"Okay, I guess. The Trexlers are a lot more uptight than we are, I guess. Twelve is a transition age, and I have a feeling Wanda would like to work free of her mom and dad. Don't quote me. I think she looks to us as a fun family. She'd do *anything* for Arvilla."

"Do you get along with the Trexlers?"

"I get along with everybody."

"Do they?"

"That I wouldn't know—if you mean do they have any enemies—anyone who would do this to them—I don't know. I'm a neighbor, not a mind reader."

"Happy family, would you say?"

"Whoa, Nellie—what *is* happy? Who is happy? It's a rough life, Bones—make no bones about that."

She thought that was awfully funny, and she filled that messy room with laughter.

"So are you saying they might not be so happy—in your opinion?"

"Well, did you see their house? Everything so perfect? It's like a museum. Can anyone be happy being so obsessed with housework?"

"What did you think when you heard Wanda was missing?"

"I didn't think anything. I thought it was a mistake and she would turn up."

"Still think so?"

"I'm an optimist."

"But where would she be?"

"Lord knows. Maybe went to the river to sort out her life."

"A twelve year old?"

"Kids mature early these days," she said, looking down at her daughter, Arvilla.

"So you weren't worried about the same thing happening to Arvilla?"

"Nah—these are one shot deals. It's got to be ransom. The Trexlers are rich. I'm not rich."

"Is your husband?"

"Ex—" she corrected me. "He does all right," she said, "but we can't hold a candle to the Trexlers."

"What does your husb—ex-husband do for a living?"

"Import-export business," she said. "He travels a lot."

"Are you in contact with him?"

"Little as possible," she said, then explained as if to the village idiot: "We didn't get along. That's why we divorced." Then, as though I'd think she was unattractive, she added, "But I have a boyfriend—Leonard Yohe."

"What does Leonard do for a living?"

"He's between jobs," she said.

"What jobs is he between?"

"He's done many things—he was a security guard—that's where I met him. He's painted houses, done gardening. Good, hard, honest work," she said defensively, "nothing glamorous."

I looked around her big house. It's a cinch he doesn't live in anything this glamorous, I thought. "So what is it keeps you from getting married?"

"My ex, for one thing."

"He doesn't like Leonard?"

"He doesn't know him. There's a clause in our divorce agreement that if I marry, Ken's alimony payments to me stop."

"Bummer," I offered, trying to be with it.

"There goes the shopping," she agreed.

"Any reservations on Leonard's part?"

She wrinkled her nose and looked at her daughter, Arvilla. "Not keen on raising someone else's kid, is the way he puts it. I think he's jealous of any attention that doesn't go his way."

"Doesn't sound good."

"No, but there are always obstacles. We'll work it out."

I thanked her for her time, and asked her to call me at the Broad Street if she had any ideas or thoughts—she said she would, but I knew she wouldn't.

Outside, as the duchess and I left the grand houses in Country Club Circle, I asked, "Why were you staring at Arvilla?"

"I wanted to see if she was telling the truth."

"Why wouldn't she tell the truth?"

"People lie sometimes," she said. That was a simple enough statement—true enough, too, unfortunately. "They don't want anybody to know what they know."

"Do you think Arvilla was lying?"

"Maybe."

"Her mother?"

"Her mother is out of it. She doesn't know if it's day or night."

"You're exaggerating," I said. "So what was Arvilla lying about?"

"I don't know exactly—but something was not right."

We walked along in silence for a while. Then as we got close to her house, she said, "Did you notice Arvilla said she *was* Wanda's best friend? She didn't say *is*. Like she doesn't think Wanda is coming back. But how would she know?"

"Oh, Duchess," I said, "you don't seriously think that Arvilla had anything to do with the fact that Wanda Trexler is missing?"

She didn't answer right away—until we got to the path to her house—then she said without looking at me—"Maybe not." Then she walked up to her front door, and turned to face me—still without eye contact she said—"But maybe so."

Six

I decided I had to talk to Clint, the duchess's grandfather, about her. This mystery stuff was killing me—"Maybe no, but maybe so." Did Clint think, I wondered, the duchess was that smart, or was she just pulling my chain?

Clint had converted the hotel barroom to an old fashioned soda fountain. Instead of beer and whiskey they offered ice cream sodas and banana splits.

As soon as he could have it painted, a sign went up over the door:

Broad Street
Soda Shoppe

Two p's and an e on shop to give it some class.

That move cost Clint a lot of money—the profit in ice cream was not what it was in alcohol, but Clint didn't care. "I have to look at myself every morning in the mirror," he said, "and I don't want any part of a business that can kill people."

Over the mirror, in back of the bar where the liquor bottles used to be, were three signs—

Drinking is not cool.
Smoking is suicide
and there are faster ways.

Drugs are for dumbells.

Clint said it was the best move he ever made. He had a place Verity could come after school and he didn't have to chase her out because she wasn't old enough. He wouldn't trade his soda fountain, he said, for all the money in the world.

Clint was just finishing breakfast when I came down, which I thought was a good thing. He'd go into the soda fountain to clean up from the night before and I could talk to him in private there. I didn't want Clara to hear.

There were only two other boarders in the place at this time. Sometimes there were more. Clint and Clara Rudy rented out the rooms with meals or not, by the night or longer. Everyone who stayed more than a night took the meals. They were cheap and Clara was a wonderful cook.

Clara brought my breakfast: Steaming coffee, ham, fried eggs, fried potatoes, pancakes with maple syrup and butter, biscuits and homemade jelly.

No one went hungry around here.

When I'd licked the last drop of the syrup from my fork, I got up and moved into the soda fountain, which was on the other side of the entry hallway. It was a large enough hallway but not as big as the lobby most hotels have. The Broad Street was not a big hotel, but it was big for Ephesus.

Clint was behind the counter washing glasses. Clint was a large man with a load of lard on his bones that would have slowed down a bear. My idea is it is impossible to be in the same room as his wife's food and not weigh as much as an elephant. But that's just my opinion.

"Morning, Clint," I said, parking myself on a stool in front of him.

"And the same to you," he said, giving me a short but friendly smile. Clint was a friendly sort of guy. It was good for his business—and good for his politics. He was never a candidate for any office, but he was a party committee man and was big behind the scenes. He had helped get his daughter, Verity's mom, elected Justice of the Peace—that was like being a judge in our town—and that's how I got to know her and Verity. She was nice to everybody. Never one to put on superior airs.

"Well, Clint," I said, "what do you make of this missing girl business?"

"Bad business," he said.

"I figure three possibilities—one, kidnapping, for money...most likely, I'd say. Two, she ran away from home. Three, someone kidnapped her to hurt her—or to hurt her parents."

Clint was polishing glasses and holding them up to the light while I talked to him, but he was listening and looking at me the rest of the time.

"Nobody seems to think she ran away from home," I said. "Home wasn't that bad for her, and they all say she isn't the type."

Clint shook his head again. "Kids nowadays...I

don't understand 'em. In my day we had to work—up early, milk the cows, go to school, study, hoe the fields. Now they have it easy. Too much free time to get into mischief."

"Do you know Wanda Trexler?"

"Seen her. Her folks bring her in for dinner once in a while."

"Anything different about her?"

"Not so I could tell. Has good manners, maybe a little spoiled, but I seen worse."

"Think it could have been a woman, kidnapped Wanda?"

"Doubt it," Clint said, still polishing away on his soda glasses. He must have had the cleanest glasses in Leighton County. "Women don't usually go in for that kind of nonsense."

"Do you know Wanda's parents?"

"Elsie and Hank?" He nodded. "He belongs to the Rotary Club."

Clint had started a Rotary Club that had lunch once a week, on Thursdays, in his hotel dining room. It was to help his lunch business. Now forty or so of the local bigshots belonged, and maybe twenty-five or so showed up for lunch every week. Pop Christman, the high school music teacher, led the singing; they had a speech and filled up on Clara's mashed potatoes, pot roast, and apple pie à la mode. There was a lot of backslapping and handshaking and good feelings all around. And Clint was right there with them, seeing that everyone had a good time and enough butter for their mashed potatoes.

"What kind of guy is Hank?" I asked. "Dr.

Hank, isn't it?"

"Yes it is. He doesn't push the doctor stuff, some call him Doc, some Hank."

"What do you call him?"

"Doctor. I think he likes it," Clint said. "He's a little stiff for me, but a nice enough fella. You got to figure he's a lot more educated than most of the group, and he's got a lot more money, but he tries to be one of the boys."

"Likes his daughter, does he?"

"I don't see anything to the contrary."

"What about this Easterbrook fella?"

"Ken? He was in Rotary before he moved out."

"Good guy?"

"Oh yeah. Had ants in his pants. Always traveling. I never understood what was so great about all those places he went—I mean all over the *world*. I guess he knows how to live, but me, I got everything I need right here in Ephesus. But Ken, he liked to keep on the move." He leaned over the counter in confidence, "I can't say if I'd been married to that ex-wife of his, I wouldn't have been running all over the globe myself."

"A tough customer?"

He pointed a finger at his ear and made the circling motion to tell me he thought she was crazy.

"Well, Clint, I want to tell you that granddaughter of yours is a pistol."

"Yeah, she's something else," he said. "Bright as a whip, you know—can spell any word God ever made up. Gets all A's in school."

"Yeah," I said.

"That thing she's got, that condition—Asheimers or something."

"Asperger's," I said. I think Clint knew what it is called, it was just his way of making it seem unimportant.

"Yeah, whatever you call it, I used to think it was too bad—you know, it's a physical thing—you can't read her writing, she has trouble throwing a ball, but I figure what good's a girl who can throw a ball—who needs it?"

"Yeah."

"And she talks in that monotone and doesn't look you in the eye," Clint went on, licking his lips and pinching his eyes half shut as if he were trying to heal Verity with the power of his thoughts. I thought I saw a tear coming to his eye. Not tough-as-nails, old Clint, I thought, but there it was—unmistakable. "I just love her," he said, all choked up. "Best thing I ever did—fix up this place so she could come to it."

At that moment the front door of the hotel opened and the duchess breezed in lugging her backpack full of books, which I swear seemed heavier than ever.

"Did you hear the news?" she said, and before I could answer, she added, "Arvilla Easterbrook is gone too. That's two girls gone."

Seven

"This is a new kettle of fish," I said to the duchess. We were sitting at a small round table in the soda fountain where Clint had sported us to dishes of chocolate ice cream. "Is it the same kidnapper trying to get more money, or is it some other person who got the idea from Wanda's kidnapper?"

"Maybe they ran away together," the duchess said.

"Bosh," I said. "It was two days apart."

"Maybe that was to make it look like they didn't go together."

"Twelve year olds think like that?" I scoffed.

"I just did," she said.

"Hmm—where would they run? Wanda would have had to wait two days somewhere. Where would she sleep, what would she eat?"

"I don't know," the duchess admitted. "I just wonder who will be next."

"Not you," I hastened to assure her, but how could I be sure? Maybe it was someone after the whole Girl Scout troop.

The phone rang. Clint answered it on the wall behind the soda fountain. "Yes, Tad, she's here."

He turned to the duchess. "Your mom says for

you to stay here until she comes for you. Word travels fast in this town."

Didn't I know it! I waved a hand—"She's probably got clients—tell her I'll walk Verity home."

He did and that seemed to satisfy Tad. Clint hung up and checked his inventory of polished glasses.

The duchess and I moved into the dining room. We were alone.

"What do you think, Duchess?" I said when we sat ourselves at the table.

"I don't know," she said.

"Hey, weren't you the one who said Arvilla was lying yesterday? Do you think they ran away together?"

"No."

"So what was she lying about?"

"I don't know."

"Do you think she knows what happened to Wanda?"

"I don't know."

Sometimes I didn't understand the duchess. I knew she was handicap and communicating didn't come easily, but how was I to know if she really meant what she said?

Then one of us got the idea to go see Olive Easterbrook. I think it was me—maybe it was her. I don't care who gets the credit.

So it was back to Country Club Circle, stopping off at Verity's house to drop off her backpack. Her mother wasn't too thrilled at the idea, in fact I heard some harsh words about the danger of girls her age being out. The duchess said she'd be safe with me and that made me feel good. Next thing I knew, the duchess was coming down her front step and we were off to the Easterbrook house.

The same music was coming from the back of the house. It was like they never turned it off.

We knocked and the door was pulled open with a sudden thrust, and from the look of Olive Easterbrook she didn't know the music was on.

"Oh, it's you," she said, and I couldn't tell how she meant it, until she said, "What do you want?"

"Just to help you find your daughter," I said, and she broke into tears.

We watched her sob for a minute—the duchess with a deadpan and me with a pan that wasn't much more alive.

"May we come in?" I said. Or maybe it was the duchess. Anyway, Olive turned and we followed her into her living room where she threw herself on a couch piled with clothes and magazines of the *People* type.

"I can't take this," she said. "I *need* this? There is no justice in the world."

I could relate to that, and I said so. She seemed pleased.

"And to think just yesterday I said no one would want her she was so ornery." And she sobbed some more. "Oh, ohooo, it's so *hopeless*—the police were just here—they weren't very encouraging. They don't even know if it's related to Wanda disappearing. There are too many crazy men in this world," she said.

"Tell me, what's the last thing you remember?"

"It was just like any other day. She left the house at the very last minute and she said, " 'Love ya, Mom!" and Mom broke down again, blubbering like a child.

"Can we see her room?" the duchess asked, and Mrs. Easterbrook seemed startled at the request.

"Well, what for? I mean, it's okay with me, but what are you looking for?"

I stepped in. I thought the duchess was out of her depth with this woman. "You never know," I said. "You get ideas, hints from things you find."

"Well, the police were up there and they didn't find anything, just some silly scratchings that kids do."

"Scratchings? What kind?"

"Oh, I don't know what it's supposed to be. Go see for yourself."

We went upstairs and found the bedroom in shambles. I had visions of the police just tearing the place apart.

"*Cops* do that?" I asked.

She shook her head. "Arvilla did it. She was not a neatnik."

"Yeah," I said, looking at the duchess. It was her idea we come up here so I wanted to see what she had in mind.

She looked around and bent down on her knees and started rifling through the papers. I could see what Arvilla's mother meant—looked like a lot of chicken scratching to me. But the duchess stared at it as though it were a language she understood.

"May I take some of these?" she asked Mrs. Easterbrook.

Olive Easterbrook shrugged. "I don't know what you want with them—the police didn't ask to take them. Help yourself."

The duchess gathered up a bunch of papers, then looked on Arvilla's shelf and took down the Girl Scout manual. She opened the front cover, then leafed through the pages—where she found another paper that seemed to catch her attention.

"This too?" she asked Olive, who was becoming mighty curious by now.

"If you can tell me why."

"I don't know yet. I'm going to try to figure it out."

"Fair enough," Olive Easterbrook said, and we went back downstairs. She was ready to show us out when I said—"Could you stand a few more questions?"

She gave a heavy sigh—"Oh, I suppose. Why did this have to happen to me?"

I thought it happened to Arvilla, but I didn't say so. I didn't want to be thrown out.

"Ms. Easterbrook," I began gently. My years on the force taught me you catch a lot more flies with honey than you do with a fly swatter. "Have you talked to your husband about this?"

She shook her head. "I tried to call him. His secretary said he was out of the country and she didn't know how to reach him—but he called in all the time and she'd ask him to call me. I told her in no uncertain terms it was a real emergency and to have him call at all costs. But I doubt he will."

"Why not?"

"Oh, he's in Bermuda or someplace like that

and he can't ever be bothered. He probably won't even know it happened, and when he gets the message, *if* he gets it, he will just think I'm being hysterical. Exaggerating again. He says I have a long history of it."

"How about your boyfriend. Leonard, is it?"

"I don't know *where* he is. Probably out job hunting. I left a message on his voicemail, but he hasn't called back yet."

"You don't think either one had anything to do with it, do you?" I know I shouldn't have asked a leading question like that, but I was more interested in her reaction—her body language—than I was with her answer. Just put the idea out there, and the more startling the better, and watch her face. Did she seem startled, or had the idea occurred to her before?

She seemed surprised. "But—but why? Why would either one want to take her? My ex wasn't high on kids—we didn't have a battle over custody—he could have her anytime he wanted her—I am not a possessive person."

"And Leonard?"

"But he doesn't *need* to kidnap her. He can see her anytime he wants. I mean, she's right *here* for heaven's sakes."

Logical. Everything she said was logical, and yet I wondered.

"Besides," Olive said, "what would he have to do with it? Two kids—best friends, neighbors—in two days. Doesn't it have to be connected?"

"Not necessarily," I said. "Not directly. The fact one happened after the other could mean the same person took them for the same reason."

Olive shuddered. "That means harm. I have no money for ransom. Neither does Leonard."

"But your ex—doesn't he have some money?"

She nodded, slowly, as though she were considering a new thought. "But nothing like this."

"Two for the price of one," I said. "Then too, it could just be a copycat thing. Someone took Wanda for one reason—giving snatcher number two the idea. Much as we like to rule out evil men, I don't think we can."

She shuddered again as the phone rang. She leaped up to get it—"Hello—oh, Leonard, thank goodness you called. Where have you *been?*...Oh, well, good—have you heard what happened? Oh yeah, I should have known it would be on the radio and TV. Leonard—I can tell you, I don't *need* this now. Can you come over—oh thanks—" she hung up.

"He's on his way," she said to no one in particular. "Called from his cell phone. He's been on job interviews so he heard it on his car radio—so I'm going to have to ask you to leave," she said standing. "I do appreciate your help—and I like you better than the police because you tell me things. They are all closed mouth."

"Couldn't I stay and talk to Leonard?" I said, emphasizing the 'I,' thinking Olive would be reluctant to have the kid around.

"Oh, no," she said. "He's very private. He'd go ape if he knew I had talked to you."

"Well," I said, "okay, but we're on your side."

"Yes, yes," she said, pushing us through the

door. "Now *go!*"

On our way to the duchess's house, I said to Verity, "What do you think? Either of those men involved?"

She shrugged her shoulders. "Don't know," she said.

"Say, what did you pick up in Arvilla's bed-room?"

"Just some...stuff."

"What kind of stuff?"

"I'll have to see if I can figure it out, first."

"Figure what out?"

"I think it's codes."

"Codes?"

"You know, kids write in codes sometimes, so the parents won't know what they are saying."

"Oh, well," I thought there was very little chance the duchess could figure out a code. "Want me to help you with it?"

"No thanks," she said, as we came to her house, "but if I need your help, I'll let you know—" and she seemed to vanish through her front door.

Eight

That duchess was something else! Where she got the idea she could crack a code without the help of an adult, I'll never guess. She's twelve years old, for heaven's sakes!

When she was safe inside her house, I thought of going back to the Easterbrook's to see what Leonard Yohe had to say for himself. But I thought that would only make Olive angry and she'd never tell us anything again.

I was talking to Clara before dinner and she told me something about Verity I didn't know. The duchess comes to the hotel after school automatically whether she has any reason or not. It's part of Asperger's—fixed routines, not always logical. I hadn't paid any attention to that before. Sometimes I was there when she was, sometimes not. And she never came on weekends. And since I left the force, I have trouble remembering what day it is.

Now that I had a case to work on, and I was making her feel good by letting her help, I was more aware she was there. And she seemed to stay longer.

When I laughed and told Clara the duchess had picked up scraps of paper in Arvilla Easterbrook's room and was planning to solve the mystery by cracking the code, Clara didn't laugh—instead she said, "Don't underestimate that little girl. She has a very special brain and she just might surprise you—what she can do."

Well, I wasn't going to be surprised—that much I knew.

I was sitting at the dining room table reading the local paper's account of the missing girls, and I thought the paper was missing something, when this tall guy came into the room. It looked like he had just come into daylight after being underground in the dark. He was so thin and floppy he reminded me of wet spaghetti. If you ever tried to stand a piece of wet spaghetti on its end you have an idea of this guy. He looked at me, then came over as fast as his noodle legs would carry him.

"Are you Bones Fatzinger?" he asked, like he was accusing me of a crime.

I admitted I was. He slumped in a chair across the table and I was relieved that he'd gotten off his feet before he collapsed.

He looked relieved too. "I'm Leonard Yohe," he said, sticking out a hand.

I took it, making sure I didn't mash his noodle fingers. "Olive said you wanted to talk to me—"

"Oh, well, geez…yes, I do, but…I mean…thanks for coming—I never thought you would."

"Well, why not? I got nothing to hide."

"So, what do you know?"

"Nothing. I got this message while I was on an interview. Olive was so hysterical, I could hardly understand her."

"Did you get the job?"

"They're going to let me know."

"What kind of job?"

"Baggage handler at the airport."

I nodded.

"Hey, don't tell me you suspect *me* of something?"

"Why would I do that?"

"Well—I don't know. Something in your tone, I guess."

"Didn't mean anything. Can you give me any hints what might have happened?"

"Somebody took her. Has to be kidnapping. But if it is, they got the wrong girl. Wanda Trexler, yes, Arvilla Easterbrook, no. The money isn't there."

"Her father? Isn't he pretty well off?"

"You couldn't prove it by me," he said. "I mean, he supports Olive and Arvilla okay, I guess, but not big bucks."

"You think Dr. Trexler has that much money?"

"Well, compared to what? Most people in town—for sure. He's not in any national billionaires club, if that's what you mean."

"How much ransom do you think he could pay?"

"No idea," he said, "more than me."

"So if you were planning a kidnapping like this, how would you do it?"

"*Me?* I wouldn't have the least idea. The thing that gets me—in Arvilla's disappearance as well as Wanda's, nobody saw anything. All these houses have windows on the street. Nobody heard any screaming or fighting. It's got to be someone the girls know."

"Same person—each girl?"

"Well it sure is similar."

"You're familiar with copycat crimes?"

"Well sure, you think I'm a dummy?"

"Certainly not. Just trying to get your ideas."

"I wish I had some ideas. Olive doesn't either."

"No enemies—you or Olive?"

"Hey, everybody has people don't like them. Me more than Olive, probably."

"Why you?"

"Got in scrapes—have some strong opinions."

"Physical fights?"

"Nothing major. Cut up a couple guys," he said, "but hey—it's not my kid they took."

"May be getting back at you."

"Wrong way. To tell the truth," he leaned toward me and whispered, "I'm not that crazy about the kid. I mean, it's no skin off my nose she's gone— you quote me and I'll call you a liar."

"So maybe you had her taken."

"Ah—phew—" he sank back in his chair and blew some air through his lips to let me know how crazy that idea was. "I came here as a courtesy to you. But I can see this is getting us nowhere."

"Where did you expect it to get us?" I could ask hardball questions with the best of them.

"Man, I don't know."

At that moment, the duchess walked in, lugging her backpack. It couldn't have been a worse time. I was finally making Leonard Yohe uncomfortable enough to blurt out a confession and in walks the kid—a wet dishrag if I ever saw one.

I signaled frantically with my face for her to get lost, but she didn't get the message. Instead, she took her book bag off her back and dropped it on the table. Social graces were not her strong point. She sat down next to me and said nothing.

"Oh, hi, Verity," Leonard said. "How's it going?"

"Good," she said.

"That's good. You know this joker?" he says, pointing to me.

She nods. Not exactly a ringing recommendation but it seemed to make Leonard think better of me.

"Trying to hang this thing on me," he said, shaking his head. I could see the two of them ganging up on me.

"That's not so," I said.

"Leonard didn't do anything," the duchess announced as though she were sitting on the throne with the queen of England. Maybe I should start calling her queen. It was important for Leonard to keep in mind Verity was only a kid and the opinions expressed by her were only those of the kid and they didn't necessarily reflect the views of the ex-cop by her side. *Adult* ex-cop, I might add. I'm almost four times her age.

"Okay, Miss know-it-all," I said, "pray, tell us why you know Leonard had nothing to do with Arvilla's disappearance."

She didn't say anything right away, just looked kind of blank, as though she had some big knockout secret she wasn't sure she could share. Then, as though seeing something on his face that made up her mind, she leaned over and unzipped her backpack, looked inside, moved her hand back and forth for something, then pulled out a spiral-bound notebook. From between some of the pages she took the sheets of nonsense words she found on Arvilla's bedroom floor.

"Here," she said, pushing the paper across the table at Leonard, "read this."

We both watched his face as he stared at the jumble of letters. "What's this?" he asked, and I think he was confused.

"A letter from Arvilla."

"To who? Why this is nonsense—where did you get this?"

"In her room," the duchess said. If Leonard was trying to scare her, it wasn't working.

"Well, this obviously doesn't mean anything. Maybe she was practicing writing her letters."

"No," the duchess said firmly, "it means something."

"What?" Leonard asked. "Do you know?"

"Yeah, Duchess, do you know?" I asked.

"I know it says something."

"But you don't know what?" I asked.

"Not yet."

"Oh," I said, my patience wearing thin. Sometimes, I swear she didn't know the difference between kids (her) and adults (us). She just sat there with her scribbles from Arvilla's room and pretended to be one of us. I guess I was a little sarcastic when I said, "Maybe when you know what it says, you'll tell us."

"Maybe," she said. I didn't like the sound of

that. I was investigating the case and she was along as more or less a charity. Like I *need* a twelve year old to help out with the rough stuff. I'm not saying she didn't have her uses, most important her connection with the two girls that had disappeared. But if she thought those scribbles meant anything—well, I don't want to say her efforts and theories were worthless—but come on! Really! This sort of thing you can fantasize about if you are young. We seasoned pros know better.

"Well, I imagine it's just a matter of time until you both get ransom notes."

"If Olive lives that long," Leonard said. "She's beside herself with grief—blames herself—says she's a terrible mother."

"She's not," the duchess said. Sometimes I just wanted to clamp my hand over her mouth—but this time I got a surprise. Leonard lit up like a Christmas tree and said, "Oh, Verity, Olive will be so happy to hear you said that. This is just terrible—if you can imagine anything worse than a mother's child disappearing."

"How would you react to a ransom note?" I asked Leonard.

"Not good, we don't have that kind of dough, but I think Olive would be relieved. We'd have something to investigate—some idea Arvilla might still be alive."

"Well, take it from a pro—maybe the cops won't tell you this now, but it would help if you talked it over—see how much money you can raise—get a loan on the house in Country Club Circle. Do you have a house?"

"No, I rent."

"Well, the idea is, when you finally get the ransom note—the demands the kidnappers make—you don't waste precious time stewing over what to do. You get the FBI right away and it's best to follow their instructions."

"But what if we can't raise the money?"

"If you get a note, or a call, you might want to go to the press—the right kind of newspaper article and you could probably raise the ransom."

"I don't know if Olive would go for that. She has her pride, you know."

"Well, whatever—it's up to you. But take my word for it, you'll get a demand for money—so will the Trexlers, so it won't hurt you to be prepared."

That's when our Duchess spoke up: "There isn't going to be a ransom note," she said.

Sometimes that kid just drove me up the wall.

Nine

After Leonard left the hotel, I had a heart-to-heart talk with the duchess.

"Duchess," I said, "I know you mean well, but I'm trying to solve a difficult case. I have to talk to adults—gain their confidence—I can't do that if you are always saying the opposite of what I say."

She didn't say anything. She was stonewalling me. Building a stone wall between us. The duchess was good at that.

"Okay, be that way," I said. "I'm not going to be able to include you if you don't do as I say."

"All right," she said. "Then I won't include you."

"Me? In what do you include me?"

"I got you into the girls' houses. I told you what was going on all the time. I was going to let you in on the code breaking, but I guess you don't care about that."

"Hey, Duchess, give me a break. I'm not saying that. But don't you think code breaking is a little out of the depth of a twelve year old?"

"Not if the people who made it were twelve year olds."

That was a zinger, all right, so I didn't argue the point. As I've often said, arguing with the duchess was time wasted. And in missing persons every minute was important.

"Do you want to help with the code?"

She caught me flat-footed. I knew nothing about cracking codes, but I was sure she didn't either. If I said no thanks, she might not have shared anything with me, and it would look to Verity as though I were afraid. On the other side of it, I was the adult, and no child should be giving me directions.

"I might do some work on the codes," I said— "if I think there's anything in it."

"We have to understand the code before we can know if there's anything that will help find Wanda and Arvilla."

She fumbled around in her backpack and pulled out a bunch of papers. "Here," she said. "I made copies. I'm working on it and so is Calvin."

"Who's Calvin?"

"A guy in my class. He's good at stuff like this."

"What stuff? He does codes?"

"Yes, he does," she said. "He makes them up all the time. Lots of them. He said he'd help."

Another kid, I thought, that's all I need. But I agreed the three of us would meet at the hotel tomorrow after school and talk about our ideas for breaking the code.

I walked the duchess home. No way should any girl be out on these streets alone. When I dropped her off on her doorstep, I hurried back to the hotel. I wanted to get right to the codes.

I spread the code papers out in front of me on the corner dining room table. I stared at the markings, but the longer I stared the more it looked like chicken scratching. A lot of letters and numbers in a disorganized and nonsensical way.

I had to admit, I had no experience with code breaking or understanding the real meaning of codes in my former career as a borough policeman. I knew you were supposed to see patterns—two or three letter words that were the same. If you saw a three letter word often and the letters were the same, you might assume the word was "the" and you'd have the "t," the "h" and the "e." But clever code makers know how to change things so they won't be that easy. For example, they could use what I thought was THE as someone's name like Sal, or a shortened name for Wanda, ARV for Arvilla, so it's no easy matter—certainly not work for children.

It got very late and Clara was closing the dining room without me having the least idea what all these scratchings meant. I took the papers to my room, kicked off my shoes, and laid on the bed, still puzzling over the meaning of it all.

The next thing I remember was opening my eyes on the dawn outside my hotel room window.

I went down to breakfast without having to change my clothes. The morning newspaper was on the table. I picked it up and read the latest account of the kidnappings. Still no notes had been received, and the police and FBI were afraid there might not be any notes. The girl's photographs were sent to all the police stations and homeless shelters in the country—

just to cover the possibility that they had run away—together or alone. Wanda and Arvilla's pictures were run in the paper again, as they had been everyday since they disappeared. The newspaper was clever in putting the pictures in different sections so even if you only read the Sports section you'd see the pictures.

I spent most of the day on the front porch. It was nice and sunny, but not too hot, so I sat myself in a rocker and set aside the codes. I realized I would not be able to understand them until it was too late for them to mean anything—if indeed they meant anything at all to start with. I realized I had to check other avenues for a solution. Secret codes between kids might be great fun, but our goal was to find and get the girls back—and all our efforts had to be directed to that end.

By the time the duchess came down the sidewalk with this strange looking kid, I had resolved very little. The news from the FBI and local police was not encouraging, and I couldn't really say I had done better. I had only left my rocking chair for lunch, and I didn't want to leave it when the duchess and her friend came up the steps and walked right by me into the hotel without saying hello or anything. I wondered if she saw me at all. I think she did, and was just not aware I was anyone she knew. That was one of the things about the duchess—she didn't react to you the way other people did.

I followed them into the dining room where they were setting up shop on the middle table. I suggested we move to the corner to be out of everyone's way, but they ignored me.

"Is this your friend?" I asked the duchess, hinting for an introduction.

"Yes," she said.

"Hi," I said to the boy, who was taking a laptop computer out of his backpack. "I'm Bones Fatzinger."

"Hi," he said, without supplying *his* name.

"What's your name?" I asked.

"Calvin."

"Oh—Calvin what?"

He didn't answer right away—then he said, "Just Calvin." He had a strange crooked smile on his thin, pink lips. He wore a tee-shirt that had been tie-dyed shades of purple and blue, rumpled short pants, and a necktie over the tee-shirt. The tie was not tied like a real necktie—more like a shoelace that didn't quite make it. His eyes were hidden behind a large pair of eyeglasses with rims like a leopard's spots.

He set up his laptop on the table—opened it and turned it on, then began speaking as though he were instructing a convention of code breakers.

"We began in the standard way, of studying the groups of letters and numbers for patterns we might recognize as common words for names—Wanda has five letters, and the second and the fifth letters are the same. Arvilla has seven letters—the first and last are not only the same, they are the same as the second and fifth letter of Wanda. So, we looked for five and seven letter words with those patterns—especially in the beginning and end of the notes. We might expect one to begin, 'Dear Wanda,' another, 'Dear Arvilla.' They might end with the names after some ending, like 'Yours in secret' or something."

"There is also the double 'l' in Arvilla," the duchess chimed in.

"Oh, yes," Calvin said. "Sometimes there is a symbol or number substituted for double letters. Two l's in Arvilla might be L2, DL for double L. Two O's in book could be eyes crossed. You can make a code anyway you want, as long as everyone who uses the code knows what it means."

"Do we know that Wanda got any of these codes? Did we ever look for anything there?" I asked, knowing the answer.

"I called Mrs. Trexler," the duchess said, surprising me with her initiative, "she said there were papers in her room like these—" she pointed at the code scratchings, "but she cleaned up and threw them away."

I groaned.

"But maybe these are *from* her, and what was thrown away were notes from Wanda."

"It's beginning to look like they ran away together, and the codes were the way they planned it and told each other about it," I said.

"Maybe," the duchess said.

"Maybe not," Nerd Calvin said. "The simplest code is to reverse the letters—A is Z and Z is A. B is Y and Y is B—" I wondered if he was going through the whole alphabet to make his point. "I programmed that and nothing came up."

"Another way is to slip a letter or a number in them. You can put the key at the beginning of the sentence in numbers. For example, start a sentence with four, and A becomes D, B is E and so forth—or you can put the four upside down, or with a zero in front or a line through it—anything to show it's different and A becomes W, B becomes V and the like."

"That's very impressive, Calvin," I said, giving the kid his due. "So what concrete conclusions have you come to? Like about what the notes mean?"

He looked glum. "Nothing yet," he said, "but Verity and I are working on it."

"How about if we turn the notes over to the FBI?"

"No!" the duchess said. "I found them—the FBI didn't do anything. I'm going to solve it."

"*You?*" I said. "This is my case."

"Well, okay," she said. "Then you solve it first. You have the same notes."

"Okay," I said. "I'll make a deal. Take one more day. If we don't have anything by then, we show the FBI. They have professionals that do this for a living. They could probably solve it in five minutes."

I couldn't get them to agree to that. It didn't matter. If they didn't solve it in one more day, *I* would take the notes to the FBI.

In the meantime, I might go back to talk to Grumbera at the local police station around the corner. Hint around. See how he felt about codes. All these scratchings from Arvilla's bedroom could be a blind alley—an alley you can go into, but there is no way out of.

"One more day," I repeated, but neither the duchess nor the nerd responded. They were too busy trying to solve the puzzle of the code.

Ten

Next morning after breakfast I went around the corner to the police station to try to find out what they thought about codes—without revealing the notes we had found at Arvilla's house.

Grumbera was on duty. He sat like Buddha in uniform behind his desk. It was a good thing the uniform was so dark, since dark colors made him look—I won't say thinner, but—less large. In white he would have looked like a mountain—in dark, only an elephant.

"Hi, Grumbera, how's it goin'?"

He looked up. I don't want to say he was asleep, perhaps just resting.

"Yeah, Bones, hanging in there."

"Good. What's the latest on the two girls?"

He shook his head. "Nothing," he said with a hopeless, tired lift of his shoulders.

"No leads?"

"We get the usual cranks and then some—but they are phonies. We check, but nothing goes anywhere."

I shook my head and eased myself into the seat across the desk from Grumbera. "The boys in uniform know anything about codes?"

"Codes? What kind of codes?" It was obvious he hadn't thought about it.

"Things two people write to each other with the words changed so only the people who know the code can understand them."

"Well, I *know* what a code is," he said, "but why do you ask?"

"Thought it might help with the case." I didn't think I was not keeping my word to the duchess and the nerd, I was just asking to get an idea of what they had done with the codes. He might help us. They might have found some and took them before we got there.

"Nah," he said. "Bunch of kid's scribbles. They didn't run away—we're sure."

"How can you be sure?"

"Well, if they were planning to run away, they would have left on the same day—how could one hide and wait for the other? And why?"

"To throw you off?"

He puffed out his lips to show me he was thinking. "We're dealing with twelve year olds. You don't expect them to be that clever."

"Maybe that's a mistake."

He thought a minute, then shook his head. "Don't think so."

I started to get up. Then I thought of something else. "Haven't there been any rewards offered?"

He looked at me with suspicion, as though I had a secret he didn't want me to have. He put his pointing finger up in front of his lips.

"It's a secret?" I asked.

He glared at me.

"But what good is a reward if no one knows about it?"

He glared at me. I had made him really angry. "Now, Bones," he said, "don't ask so many questions or I'll have to ask you to stop coming in here."

"Well, now, Grumbera, the last time I looked it was still a free country. You want to be nice to the taxpayers."

"Hah!" Grumbera said. "Since when did you become a taxpayer? Last time I looked, you were still a guest at the Broad Street Hotel. You become a property owner all of a sudden?"

"I pay room and board to Clint. He passes some of it on to the borough to pay your salary."

"Yeah, right," he said.

I decided Grumbera was getting edgy, and I'd better get out of there. I might need him in the future.

When I got back on the street, I decided to take a walk back to Country Club Circle, to see if walking the neighborhood would give me any ideas.

I walked down Second Street to enter Country Club Circle from the middle top edge of the circle. It was a pretty, sunny day in early April—not much different than the day in late March when Wanda, the first of the two girls, disappeared.

I made my way around the circle, looking for clues. The houses were far apart with enough space between them to put four downtown houses. The trees were tall, the bushes wide, so anyone could hide in them. With the houses on both sides of the street, there were only a few places between the Trexler's house and the bus stop where a car in the street could not be seen from a house. Someone could hide in the bushes, but if Wanda or Arvilla had been surprised by a stranger, everyone agrees they would have screamed and alerted at least one neighbor.

Then I noticed a space between the two girl's houses where you could walk through trees and bushes to the golf course without being seen. On one side of this natural path was the side of one house's garage with no windows. On the other side was a modern house and two stone walls set at angles—one covering a parking carport, another a woodpile and storage.

To test my idea, I walked through the path to the golf course, looking left and right as I went to be sure there were no big windows looking at me. There was enough plant screening that it would have been hard to see anyone taking that path. The homeowners had planted shrubs and trees to give them privacy from the golf course, so they couldn't see me when I came out of the path onto the course.

I crossed the course a short distance to where third street traveled down the hill to the river. There was an unused barn across the street. I checked it out. It was just an empty barn, and I couldn't see any signs of kids living there on the first step of their journey— wherever it took them. I tried to imagine Wanda, who disappeared first, hiding out in this musty barn for a couple of days while Arvilla snuck food to her, then joined her to move on, but I couldn't. Two twelve year olds were not sophisticated enough to do that. If they did run away, they must have had help.

Still, if someone kidnapped them, why didn't

they fight or scream?

I walked up Third Street to the bus stop and looked around. Nothing suspicious—no place to hide, nothing that would interfere with them being seen at the bus stop. And the kids at the bus stop had a fair view of the street Wanda and Arvilla would ordinarily walk down to get to the bus—but they couldn't see all the way to the path to the golf course I had just taken. I thought any car that took them anywhere would have headed down the hill rather than back to town. Down the hill to the river, it was pretty woodsy, and the girls could walk or ride without being seen.

On my way back to the hotel, I thought about the duchess and the nerd and wondered if they had made any progress on the code. I had given them until today to solve it or I would take it to the police and FBI for solving.

If I couldn't crack it, how could they?

Eleven

"Clara," I said after lunch, where she was eating her noon meal at a dining room table under the mural of the green grass, green trees and a couple of white sheep. "When you were a child, did you ever want to run away from home?"

"Everyday," she said with a smile. "Still do."

Clara had a neat sense of humor.

"So how did you imagine it? Where would you go? How would you live?"

"I never thought that much about it. I was just going to escape. When you're that young, you don't worry about details."

"How about when you were twelve?"

"Oh, that's a tough age. Rebellious—I wanted to be so grown up at twelve."

"Can you imagine getting in a car with a stranger at twelve?"

"Well, I hope not. But I probably wouldn't have wanted to admit I was scared—so I don't know. When you're twelve, you don't think grownups get scared, and you want to be grown up."

The duchess and her nerdy pal entered the dining room like clockwork, throwing backpacks on the table as though they owned the place.

I tried a "How's it goin', kids?" to no response.

Nerdy took out his laptop computer and set it up. Then he drew a bunch of papers out of his backpack and spread them all over the table. On the papers were drawn the alphabet frontward and backward with numbers one through nine upside down and right side up.

"What's that supposed to mean?" I asked.

"I substituted letters for the letters on the code. I did many, many 'translations' until I came on one that made sense."

"What did you find out?" I asked, not hiding the fact I wasn't going to believe what he told me.

The duchess answered. "He found an X."

"An X? What's that?"

"A secret person," she said. "He has no name, only an X."

"Or she," the nerd chimed in. "It says, 'X says this' and 'X says that'. Every sentence has a number in front of it. Sometimes the same, sometimes different from the sentence before."

"What does it say?" I asked.

"We only have a small bit," the duchess said. "But we know the code."

"I hope it's right," the nerd said.

"Does the message make sense?" I asked.

"Sort of," the nerd said. "But we are missing too much to be sure. When I put together everything we have, the message makes sense by itself, but it doesn't tell much about the bigger picture. We need more letters from Arvilla to Wanda. What we have seems to be from Wanda to Arvilla. Very short."

"What does it say?"

Here the duchess recited the message she had obviously memorized: "X is ready."

"Ready for what?" I asked.

But there was no answer to that on the secret message. I had more questions than the code breaking had answers.

"We need more messages," I said.

"Get them," the nerd said. "I'll decode them."

"How?" I asked.

The duchess answered. "Maybe we can find more in Arvilla's room." She had a good idea, which is bound to happen from time to time.

"What about Wanda's room?" I asked.

"Her mother won't let us in."

"How do you know?"

"I know her mother."

This was not encouraging. "Maybe we can trick her. Like you wander around the house like you don't know what you're doing."

"Yeah," the nerd said, "Verity can play dumb. Some people think she *is* dumb. People who don't know her." He looked at me as though he thought I was one of those who thought that she was dumb. I ignored him.

"But Mrs. Trexler is her scout leader." I turned to the duchess. "Think you can do it?"

"I can try," she said. "But her mother said she threw everything away."

The nerd went home and we walked to Country Club Circle and went to the Easterbrook house first. No one answered the door. "She's probably shopping," the duchess said.

A light bulb went on in my head. Then it went off again. I couldn't ask the duchess to break in.

"The door is probably open," she said, trying it. It was open. She looked at me. "Are you coming?"

That took care of that. I decided the duchess and Arvilla were friends and it was okay for her to visit even if she wasn't home. I followed and closed the door. "Do we have an escape plan if Mrs. Easterbrook comes home?" I asked the duchess.

"We'll hear her and go out the back door."

I followed the duchess into Arvilla's room. The room looked as it had when we were in it before. There were a few more papers that we recognized as code, but I was beginning to wonder if these codes were such secrets, why were they just lying about? Secrets should be hidden.

Did Arvilla want to be caught? Or were the codes not even related to the disappearance of the two girls? And were these codes actually sent to someone else, or was Arvilla just fooling around? And if Arvilla sent them to someone, was it necessarily Wanda?

We went through books, looked under the bed and behind the dresser, under the rug, inside her pillow, in her clothes closet. You'd think if the girls were running away they would have taken some clothes, but their mothers hadn't seen them go out of the house with anything unusual. There was no evidence either had any money—not enough to get very far and to eat and buy clothes and pay for a hotel. What happened was just a mystery.

We didn't find any more code papers until we lifted up the mattress. There was a small pile of papers with what looked like the code on them. The duchess picked them up and paged through them.

"This is the code," she said. "Look, an upside-down five. That means five from the end—so V is really A."

I took her word for it. "Let's get out of here before Olive comes back," I said, and we slipped out the way we came.

The duchess wanted to hang onto the code pages, but I thought I'd better keep them myself—she was liable to show them to Mrs. Trexler, and that wouldn't help us.

We walked down the street, and just as we got to the Trexler's door we saw a car pull up into the driveway of the Easterbrook house. A man and woman got out of the car—I thought I recognized Olive Easterbrook and her boyfriend Leonard Yohe.

I rang the doorbell at the Trexler house. Mrs. Trexler answered, and she didn't look pleased to see us.

"Oh," she said, "my husband says I shouldn't be talking to you."

I didn't like that. Nobody likes to be rejected. Nobody wants to be undesirable. "Well, Mrs. Trexler, I am trying to help you get your daughter back, and we have had some breaks—I'd like to talk to you about them."

She tightened her lips and shook her head once. Then I saw signs of weakening on her face and body. She looked at the duchess, then back at me. "I can't talk to you, but Verity is one of my scouts, so I guess you can come in with her."

"Thank you," I said, and followed her into her living room.

I sat facing her where I could see into the rest of the house. She had her back to the hallway to the bedrooms. The duchess stood behind her.

"Don't you want to sit down, Verity?" she asked.

"I'll stand," she said, to Mrs. Trexler's back.

Elsie Trexler frowned, but I started talking, to get her mind off Verity.

"We have some encouragement that the girls might be okay," I said. It was news that couldn't help but interest Elsie Trexler.

She leaned forward on the couch waiting to hear. I let her wait. "What is it?" she insisted.

"I can't tell you too much now. I don't want to jinx what we have so far, but we are looking into secret messages we believe your daughter and Arvilla Easterbrook might have exchanged. Do you know anything about that?"

"No...I..."

The duchess slipped down the hall. We thought there was a chance Mrs. Trexler would have given permission for her to enter Wanda's bedroom, but it was better not to take any chances of her not letting us.

"Have you gone to the police with your theory?" she asked. "That's what my husband would ask right away."

I shifted in my chair. This woman was an expert at making me uncomfortable. "My position with the police, being what it is," I said, "does not make it easy for me to give them advice."

"But surely they would welcome help—if it was positive—"

Surely not, I thought, but I didn't argue. "I don't work for the police anymore," I said. "I work for myself. A *private* detective," I said with emphasis. "Private detectives can often do things the police can't. Some people find value in this. If you don't, perhaps I should not bother you."

"Perhaps that would be best," she agreed.

Ordinarily on that note I would have stood and said goodbye, but the duchess was still in the bedroom and I couldn't just leave her there. So, I said, "What have the police done for you so far?"

She stiffened.

"I suppose you know they think after forty-eight hours of being missing it is not easy to find anyone...". The word I wanted to add was 'alive,' but I didn't.

"Yes," she said, hanging her head.

"They have their methods. The FBI is much more experienced than our police in kidnapping. But what if they weren't kidnapped?"

"You mean they just ran off together?"

"Yes. That's what I am investigating."

"What do you have to go on?" she asked.

"Some mysterious correspondence," I said. "I cannot tell you exactly, but I would like to be free to bring you what I have when I think it would serve some purpose."

"Certainly," she said.

"And at that time—if you think my information might be useful—you might think of...paying me something."

"Oh dear, I'm afraid the doctor handles payments and such, and as you know, he has been rather hesitant to talk to you on the matter."

"Yes, I remember," I said. "Perhaps he isn't as interested in getting Wanda back—"

That made her angry. "How *dare* you," she said, and I thought she was going to throw me out, leaving the duchess stuck in Wanda's room.

I was beginning to get nervous—the duchess was taking too long—but rushing was not one of her talents. Elsie Trexler and I stared at each other.

"Why don't we leave it at this," I said. "I will get all I can to help your case. If I find something you don't know about, I'll come to you. If you aren't interested at that time, we'll forget it."

"You'll give it to the police, then?"

"I don't think so," I said slowly, still giving the duchess more time. "If you wouldn't be interested, why would the police?"

"But, but that's not fair!" she cried.

"Is it fair if I solve the case I shouldn't be paid?"

She glared at me a moment, then said, "I'll ask my husband." She stood, wanting me to go. I took my time standing, trying to look down the hall without Mrs. Trexler catching on.

At that lucky moment, the duchess came down the hall, her face as always, showed no sign of emotion.

"Thank you, Mrs. Trexler, for seeing me," I said. "I wish you all success in finding your daughter Wanda, alive and well. If I have something for you the police can't deliver, I will let you know—and let you decide what, if anything, it is worth to you." I looked at the duchess, who was back in her original place behind Mrs. Trexler.

"Okay, Duchess, let's go."

"Oh, goodness, Verity," Mrs. Trexler said, turning around. "You were so quiet I didn't even remember you were there."

Twelve

Outside the Trexler's house, I couldn't wait to ask the duchess—"Did you get anything?"

She nodded. "I found some stuff," she said.

"Where?"

"The same place. Under the mattress."

"Did you look at it?"

"I did. Just enough to see it is the same code," she said. "Calvin can figure it out."

I didn't want to wait that long, but I didn't want to wrestle with it myself either.

"When can we get Calvin to look at it?"

"We can go to his house," she said.

"Where is it?"

"He lives around the block from me. I'll show you."

We walked up her street and turned into a side street before we got to her house. We went up the front porch of a red brick, two story house with white shutters. I rang the bell.

Master Nerd answered the door.

"Hi, Calvin," the duchess said, waving the papers she'd found in his face. "I found more code at the Trexlers—and a couple more at Arvilla's."

His eyes lit up. He loved the challenge. "Come in," he said.

We followed him through a dark hallway to a small kitchen in the back, with a table in a breakfast area. His laptop computer was open on the table. We sat down while the duchess passed the papers to the nerd, who examined them with a frown. He set them down next to his laptop and fiddled with the keyboard. Then he began typing from the papers. He was deep in concentration for so long I finally asked him, "What's happening?"

"I made a program to figure the code."

"Really?" I asked. "Does it work?"

"Sure it works," he said, not looking up. "If it didn't work, I wouldn't call it a program."

"What's it say?" I asked, pointing to the code papers.

He frowned. "There's a problem," he said.

"What's the problem?"

"This X doesn't fit anywhere. We think the X is a name, but there's no way of telling what name it is. Depending on which code the sentence uses, the X could be anything from C down through the alphabet to X itself."

"What are the other words?" I asked. "Show me your translation. Maybe I can tell you what X is supposed to be."

"I can put them sort of in order, but there is a lot missing, and I can't tell what's missing. I think the first letters are missing. Maybe some between what we have here. I don't know."

"So what does it say?" I insisted, pointing again to the papers.

He pushed his glasses that were sliding down his nose back up with a finger. "This one says, 'Do you think Billy Culp is cute?'"

"Oh," I said, very disappointed.

"Then here's the answer—'He's cute, but not as cute as Freddy Weiss.'"

"Is that all it is?" I asked. "Nothing about their disappearance? Where they went? Why?"

"One at a time," he said, frowning. "I can only do one at a time. And besides, we don't know what order they were sent in. For instance, do Billy and Freddy have anything to do with it? Are they code in a code—meaning something besides what it seems?"

I had to hand it to the nerd. He was no dummy.

The next revelation from the nerd's lips was, "'X says go.'"

"Go where?" I asked. "To gym class, to the store—home? On a trip?"

He shrugged his shoulders. He worked intently for a while at his computer. The duchess stood up and started a slow, rhythmic dance.

"Sit down, Verity," he said, "you're making me nervous."

Verity frowned and sat—twisting her hands together, pushing them back in the double-jointed way she had. I didn't blame her, I was nervous myself about what was coming out of that machine. But Nerd just kept on nerding. I suppose I could have figured the code out myself by counting letters, backwards and forwards, but it was so much easier to let the machine do it.

"Here's a short one," he said. "'X says Jake.'"

"Who is Jake?" the duchess asked.

"I don't know," said the nerd.

I didn't either. "Let's keep going," I said. "Do another one."

He bent over his machine and punched more keys on the keypad. He frowned some more. He was a good frowner. It made him look serious and important.

"Here's one," he said. "'Won't need to take anything?'"

My first thought was that meant some kind of robbery where they wouldn't have to steal anything. I said so.

"No," the duchess said. "It's that they were going away and wouldn't need to take any clothes or anything."

"They'd wear the same clothes all the time?" I asked.

"Or someone would buy them new ones."

The nerd didn't comment. He was hard at work on his computer. He stared at the screen so hard I thought his eyeballs were going to fall out. "O-z," he said. "What's o-z?"

"What's the sentence?" I asked.

"'Want to go to o-z?'"

"The Wizard of Oz," the duchess said. "It was a book—and a movie. It was a place in a dream that everyone wanted to go to become what they wanted."

"Neat," he said.

"But when they got there," the duchess said, "it

was nothing but an old guy behind a curtain, making believe he was this great wizard who knew everything, but he didn't, really."

It soon became obvious we were missing some—maybe a lot—of messages. So maybe it didn't mean anything. The nerd was smart enough to keep the messages separate so we thought we could tell who sent and who received which ones. The Oz question was sent by Arvilla. 'Won't need to take anything?' was sent by Wanda.

"Do you know the boys in the note, Duchess? Freddy and Billy?"

"Yes."

"Could you talk to them? See if they know anything that could help us?"

"What should I say?"

"Oh, just start talking about the missing girls. Then say they thought you were cute and see how they react. Can you tell from their faces if they are uncomfortable knowing something—or are surprised the girls thought they were cute? Better still, do you think you could bring them to the hotel after school, and I'll ask them?"

"I'll ask," she said.

"Can you do any of Wanda's notes to Arvilla?" I asked Calvin.

He reached down to the right of his computer and lifted a note. He had put the pages we'd found at Arvilla Easterbrook's house to the left of the computer, and those from Wanda Trexler's house at the right. He moved the top note closer, stared at it, and began punching the keys. When he finished he announced—

"This one says, 'Remember the Lion.'"

That didn't ring any bells with me. "What's that mean?"

"The Cowardly Lion in *The Wizard of Oz*," the duchess said. "I read the book. He wanted to go to the wizard to get courage. So maybe Wanda needed courage, and Arvilla told her to remember the lion who wanted courage and went to see the wizard."

"So maybe that was Arvilla telling Wanda to get some courage to do what they were going to do."

"Yeah," the nerd agreed without seeming to think about what was being said. "Wanda to Arvilla— 'The Tin Man will freak.'"

"Who? What?" I asked.

"The Tin Man didn't have a heart. He wanted to get one." It was the duchess who knew her *Wizard of Oz* the way some people knew the Bible.

"So who is she talking about?" I asked.

"I don't know," the nerd said. "I just tell you what they say."

I realized we could stay there far into the night trying to figure these unclear messages out—and maybe then we wouldn't know any more than we did at that kitchen table when the translations rolled hot off the computer.

So I said, "Let's just decode all the messages. Maybe we can put them together and make some sense of it when we have them all to consider."

"Okay," the nerd said, and, pushing his glasses

back up to the bridge of his nose, he went to work. The duchess and I watched in wonder at the working of the computer keyboard under Nerd's fingertips.

The next—found under Wanda's mattress: "'You have a Tin Man, I have a Scarecrow.'"

"Look at here," Calvin said, "this one says, 'Get away from the Wicked Witch of the West.'

"Then another, 'I can't wait for the yellow brick road!'"

We speculated the Wicked Witch was Mrs. Trexler and the yellow brick road was their planned escape—but where and how were not so clear.

"Why don't I take these and see what I can figure out?" I said.

The duchess said, "No. I found them, I want to keep them."

Calvin said, "I'll print you out a set," and he went to his bedroom to print out the pages for me.

"Good work, Calvin," I said, and the duchess and I left the way we came, to try to figure out what all these secret messages meant.

Thirteen

While I walked the duchess home, I said, "I think the codes show the girls are still alive—like they planned the whole thing. What do you think?"

"I do too. But I don't think they planned anything alone."

"Do you think Freddy and Billy have anything to do with it?"

"No," she said. "I'll ask them tomorrow, but I don't think they're smart enough."

"Why do you say that?"

"I remember how slow they were learning to read in the first grade."

"You remember a lot of details, don't you?" I asked the duchess.

She nodded.

"Do you *ever* forget *anything?*"

Was that a hint of a smile on her face? "Not that I remember," she said.

"How far back can you remember?"

"When I was a little kid."

Now I had to smile at her. To me, she was a little kid. When you're twelve, three is little.

"What's the first thing you remember?"

"Crying a lot."

"You don't mean in the hospital?"

"I don't know where—everywhere, I cried a lot."

"Why?"

"I don't know," she said. "Then when I was two and a half, I threw my mother's clothes out of the upstairs window."

"Why did you do that?"

"I don't know why," she said. "It seemed like fun."

"What did your mother do?"

"She scolded me. She looked at me funny, like she couldn't understand. My father asked me why I did it, but I didn't know—"

"How do you remember you were two and a half—instead of two or three?"

"I just remember—it was between my birthday parties."

When we got to the duchess's house, her mother was on the front porch saying goodbye to someone—one of her clients, no doubt. The man left and she hailed me—"Yo, Bones, come in for a cup of tea?"

It was a kind invitation. I didn't get many such since my falling out with the force. People were so self-righteous—and I got the feeling so many of them thought they were so much better than me. Or that was the way they had to play it. But the thing about being a cop is you find out how many people have shortcomings.

"Well, thanks," I said, and I went in for tea.

Tad was known for serving tea to her friends. I remember when she was little, she loved to have tea parties.

I knew her when, you might say. Everybody in this town knows everybody else. She always offered the cops tea when she was Justice of the Peace. To get elected to the six-year job of Justice of the Peace, you didn't have to be a lawyer, but it helped.

We called her honor, "Tad," because she was tiny. Lots of locals have nicknames—like Grumbera and Bones. I remember those days—over twenty years ago now—she was just out of law school and looked like she could still get into the movies for the kid's price. Still looked fifteen, almost thirty years younger than she was. A good-looking kid and you didn't get any baloney from her. She was good to us cops, but if we screwed up, she'd rule against us, then take us out to lunch.

She had two kids before the duchess—a pre-law student (boy), and a high school student (girl). After her six year term as Justice of the Peace was up, she set up shop in her home where she did legal work for the locals—wills and estates mostly—nothing that would take her out of the nest while she was raising her kids.

I sat on her couch while she went to the kitchen to make the tea. The duchess ran upstairs to her room.

Soon there was a loud banging from above, like heavy objects hitting the floor.

When Tad came in with the tea, I asked,

"What's that noise upstairs?"

"Oh, just Verity dancing."

She sat and poured the tea from a cute teapot that was one of her collection. This one was shaped like a kitten. She set down a plate of cookies in front of me.

"So," she said, sitting opposite on a loveseat—a couch for two—"you are working on the disappearance of the two girls—any progress?"

"I think so," I said, carefully. Though I considered Tad a friend, I didn't want to spill all the beans—she could go to the neighbors or the families of the victims and spoil what we had done so far.

The racket from upstairs died down. "How well do you know the Trexlers and Easterbrooks?" I asked.

"Not well—Elsie Trexler is Verity's scout leader, and I'm grateful she does it. Otherwise I'd be stuck with it—the other mothers work outside the home. The Trexlers are pleasant, successful people as near as I can tell—Mrs. Easterbrook is divorced, and has a boyfriend."

"Do you have any theories on the missing girls?" I asked.

"Not really," she said, "I am not as certain as the mothers that they didn't just run away. And I know Arvilla as a great kidder, so she just might have gotten it into her head that running away and scaring the daylights out of her mother would be good fun."

"Wanda too?"

"Wanda's another story. I don't think she would do something like this on her own." She frowned. "But I'm not convinced things are as peachy as they seem in that household. Everything is too perfect, you know what I mean?"

"No, I…"

"Oh, appearances are very important."

"Aren't they always?"

"Oh, yes, I guess," I said, "but they seem more so there. A successful doctor, the wife who doesn't have to work and is always so beautifully dressed. Does her volunteer work with a smile—scout leader, Red Cross, symphony. And Wanda is an only child so she is the focus of all their child rearing. Don't get me wrong, it's a nice setup, I just sometimes wonder—"

"If it's too perfect?"

"Could be," I said, taking a drink of some fruity kind of tea. I held the cup up to Tad—"Good," I said.

"Thanks," she said. "Passion fruit."

"Oh," I said, not being terribly familiar with passion fruit. "Say, I was wondering, about Verity. See, I don't really understand what she's got."

There was more pounding upstairs—almost as though she were commenting. "She can't hear what I'm saying, can she?" I asked.

"No."

"So that's not a reaction…?"

"No," she smiled. "She just feels like dancing sometimes."

"Oh, well, you know this whole thing started at the Broad Street Hotel. She seems to come there everyday after school. I guess so she won't be in your way."

"No," she smiled, "she's never in my way—she goes up to her room on the rare occasion I have a client here. I have most of them in when she's in school. She just likes to go to see Clint and Clara. They give her ice cream and cookies. Habits are strong with Asperger's."

"It's rather nice," I said. "Anyway, I like her— and I look forward to her visits—and I let her help with the case, though I don't know what help I could get from a twelve year old."

She smiled and poured another cup. "Well, if she's ever in your way, just tell her—she'll back off."

"Oh, no," I said, "she helps with little things, like she knows the Trexlers and Mrs. Easterbrook. And she has this nerdy friend who is a whiz with a computer." So I got to thinking, maybe she *was* helping me more than I realized.

"More tea?"

"No, thanks."

She poured it in my cup anyway.

"You know, there is something I wanted to ask, if I may."

She smiled, sipping her hot tea. "You may ask anything, Bones. That doesn't mean I have to answer it."

"Oh, yes, right—sometimes the duch... Verity..."

"That's okay," she said. "I think it's charming you call her the duchess."

"Oh—thanks," I said. "Anyway, sometimes she'll say she reads these books that I don't see a twelve year old reading. And she'll tell me everything in them—like she'd just read them today—is she pulling my chain?"

"Oh, no, Verity wouldn't...pull your chain, as you say. Everything with her is straightforward."

"So I can believe what she says about stuff she's read?"

"You can take it to the bank," Tad said.

I thanked her for the tea and the chat, and made my way back to my hotel home.

That night I looked at all the random sentences to make sense of them, if I could. I didn't spend much time in my small room, but I didn't want anybody to see what I was doing and get suspicious. Maybe ask me a lot of questions. Maybe get so nosey they take their suspicions to the police. All I needed was for the police to take over the codes. They'd probably turn them over to the FBI, and that would be the end of my involvement in the case.

I wanted to solve the case before the police did so they would see the mistake they made kicking me off the force...maybe they'd realize they should take me back.

They could do a lot worse.

Fourteen

I had trouble sleeping that night. My head was swimming with thoughts of the Wizard of Oz, trying without success to make sense of the messages Calvin had decoded.

In the morning at breakfast, Clara asked me for my rent. I told her I was expecting to be paid for this big job I was working on, but she didn't believe me.

That unpleasant encounter made me think of Dr. Trexler. He was really my only hope of getting money—he was the only one rich enough to pay. The trouble was he didn't seem to like me and only wanted to work through the police, which I thought was his way of telling me I was no longer a policeman. Rubbing it in.

My best shot, I thought, was through the wife—Elsie Trexler. I had to go to see her, and while I was out in the rich section I had a question to ask Olive Easterbrook too.

It was before ten in the morning when I arrived at the Easterbrook house. I didn't expect Olive would be out shopping because the stores weren't open yet.

When she came to the door, long after I rang the bell the second time, she was still in her night-gown with a bathrobe thrown carelessly over it.

She looked disappointed. Was she expecting Santa Claus in April? "Do you have any news?" she asked eagerly.

"We're working," I said.

"Want to come in?"

"Oh, no thanks—I won't bother you so early. I was just wondering if you could put me in touch with your ex-husband?"

"Hah!" she gave a short laugh like a pistol shot. "Good luck."

"Does he have an office—any way to contact him in emergencies?"

"He doesn't *want* to be contacted," she said with a frown. "That's the whole point. He has an office with a part-time secretary."

"Where is it?"

"In Allenville," she said, "—on Seventh Street, I believe. If you ever find him there, you'll be luckier—or *unluckier*—than I ever was."

"When is the secretary there?"

"Search me. Whenever she feels like it. He's never there to check on her."

But she gave me the address, and went back into the house, probably to get dressed for shopping.

I moved down the street to ring the bell at the Trexler house. Mrs. Trexler opened the door, beautifully dressed as always. I couldn't be sure, but it looked like a cashmere suit to me, some beige tone.

"Hello," she said, as cold as a Frosty Freeze.

"Hi—" I tried to inject some warmth, "—May I come in?"

She frowned. "My husband doesn't want me

talking to you." She was like a broken record on the subject.

"But why not?" I asked. "If I am trying to find your daughter—where's the harm?"

She frowned again, but apparently saw the logic. "Okay," she said. "But please, you mustn't stay long."

I followed her into her neat-as-a-pin living room, where we sat in our usual places.

"I have to ask you a favor," I began.

She raised her eyebrows as though the granting of a favor to a guy as low on the totem pole as I was, was out of the question. "What kind of favor?"

"I have an idea I can find your daughter—alive and well—but I don't have the financial wherewithal to do it on my own."

"Money?" she said, with a slanted eye. "How much do you need?"

I licked my lips. Was I getting close? "I think two thousand should give me a start. If I bring her home I wouldn't object to getting a little more than my expenses as a reward."

"But," she said, having a sudden idea, "you didn't kidnap her yourself, did you?"

"Oh, Mrs. Trexler—please. I'm trying to help you. I was an officer of the law. I don't do kidnapping. I don't do crime of any kind. How could you think so?"

"Well, you claim to know where she is. How would you?"

"I'm doing an investigation."

"And you know something the police and the

FBI don't?"

I nodded.

"Shouldn't you tell them?"

I shook my head. "Kidnapping can be a very delicate thing. If you aren't careful, the victim can wind up dead. I don't want to take the chance of one of those large organizations messing it up."

"I'll talk to my husband," she said.

"I was hoping you wouldn't have to do that. Your husband doesn't seem to want to work with me. I think that's a mistake. When something like this happens you should be willing to work with any reputable person. Why leave any stone unturned?"

"But I don't have money of my own. I'd have to get it from my husband, even if I were convinced you had something."

"I have something—hot—I assure you."

"Well, you haven't shown any evidence."

"I'm not at liberty to talk about it just yet."

"Yes, I understand—all right—I'll try to convince the doctor we should take a chance on you. We both want Wanda back—I don't have to tell you that—I'll be in touch."

Back at the hotel, I called the number Olive Easterbrook had given me for her ex-husband's office. I got an answering machine and left my number and asked to be called back.

I sat in the dining room, before lunch, and wrote and rewrote the messages the girls had sent each other, trying to get some ideas from them.

I must have been stewing over the case less than an hour when Clint came into the room to tell me I had a phone call.

I took it in the soda fountain.

"Hello?"

"Hi," a woman's voice said. "This is Nellie—I'm Mr. Easterbrook's secretary. You called?"

"Yes, thanks for calling back. I wanted to talk to Mr. Easterbrook. Do you know where I can reach him?"

"Oh, no, I don't."

"Well, I'd like to drop over to see you."

"What for?"

"Just to get some information."

"Well, I'm not in the office much," she said. It sounded like they were both in hiding.

"How about now?" I said.

"Now?"

"Are you in your office now?"

"Yesss…" she answered, as if she didn't want to.

"I'll be right over," I said.

"But…"

I didn't give her a chance to get out of it, I just hung up.

Fifteen

Her name was Nellie Nelson, and she held down the fort in Easterbrook's office on a busy street in Allenville, the closest city to Ephesus.

Nellie was a nice looking woman, probably a little older than she would have liked. It was not a large office—two rooms, one for the boss, and one for Nellie. Great pains had not been taken in decorating it. Right away I noticed *Wizard of Oz* pictures on the wall.

"What can I do for you?" Nellie asked in a way that told me I might be ruining an otherwise perfect day.

"I'd like to talk to your boss," I said. "Can that be arranged?"

"He's not here."

"I know that. But can I call him?"

"I don't have a number for him."

"Does he call in?"

"Yes."

"Could I talk to him when he does?"

"I never know when that's going to be."

"How often does he call?"

"Depends."

"On what?" Getting an answer from her was like pulling teeth.

"Where he is. He travels a lot."

"Doing what?"

"He's in import-export."

"What kind of goods?"

"Any kind he can make money on. You name it."

"Give me an example."

"Oh, he'll buy dresses in Mexico and India, wood carvings in Africa, jewelry in Malaysia, bananas in Ecuador, diamonds in Russia—anything."

"Wow!" I said. "Have you talked to him about his missing daughter?"

"Yes, a few times."

"What does he say?"

"He's very upset."

"Did he ever say he would come home to help look for her?"

"He would, of course, if he thought he could help. But he does want to know everything that's happening on the case."

"What do you tell him is happening?"

"Not much. I read him the newspaper accounts. The twenty-five thousand dollar reward that was just in the paper. He knows about that."

That was what Grumbera had been so secretive about.

"Where did he call from last?"

"Barbados."

"Does he have a cell phone?"

"If he does, I don't know about it."

"You're his *secretary*?"

"Yes."

"How long?"

"Going on six years now."

"And you don't know if he has a cell phone?"

"No."

"*When* did he call last?"

"A couple of hours ago."

"Will he call again today?"

"Doubt it."

"Tomorrow?"

"Maybe—you never know."

"Would you give him my number and tell him I urgently need to talk to him about his daughter?"

"I can give him your number—but he's not very good about returning calls."

Great, I thought. "Can you tell me what kind of relationship he has with his daughter?"

"Being a father has never been his focus."

"What is?"

"Work. Travel. Trying to make money."

"Does he make a lot of money?"

"I wouldn't say so. He makes a living. But his line is very competitive."

"Think someone might ask him for ransom?"

"Might. But he pays a lot of alimony to his ex-wife, Olive, and child support too."

I had a sudden idea. If the girl disappeared for good, he would save on his child support. I hoped no father would consider that, but it did pop into my head.

"Oh, by the way," I asked, "what are all these pictures of the *Wizard of Oz* doing on the walls?"

"Oh, Mr. Easterbrook has a thing about the *Wizard of Oz*. It's his favorite movie. Seen it umpteen times. He gives people nicknames from the movie."

"For instance?"

"His ex-wife, for instance—he calls her the Scarecrow."

"Because she's thin?"

Nellie giggled. "No, because the Scarecrow was going to Oz to look for a brain."

"Oh," I said. "Not very nice."

"No," she said, "but maybe not so far off the mark."

"What does he call you?"

"Me—I'm the Cowardly Lion."

"Why?"

"He thinks I need courage."

"Do you?"

"Maybe."

"For what?"

"Can't say—my secret."

"Who is he?"

"Oh, he's the Wizard."

"Because he's make-believe?"

She shrugged. "Ask him."

"I'd like to—you're going to have him call me?"

"I'll ask."

"How about his daughter? Arvilla? Who is she?"

"Dorothy—she's looking for the Wizard too—to get back home to Kansas," she said. "Did you know that was her middle name?"

"No."

"He wanted it to be her first name, but his wife put her foot down, so they named her after Olive's mother."

"Hmm—any other characters come to mind?"

She frowned. "Well, there's the Tin Man, who wants a heart."

"Who's that?"

"Anybody he thinks is cold."

"Anybody in particular?"

"Not that I know of."

I emphasized that Mr. Easterbrook should call me if he had any interest in finding his daughter.

"Do you have her?"

"No," I said.

"Who shall I say you are with?"

"What? I'm alone."

"The police, the FBI—what's your interest?"

"I'm a private investigator."

"Working for whom?"

"Whoever will hire me."

"Who did on this case? Mrs. Easterbrook? The other family?"

I smiled a mysterious smile. "That would be telling," I said.

We said goodbye, and I got the feeling she wasn't sorry to see me go.

In the car during the four or five mile ride from Easterbrook's office to the Broad Street Hotel, I tried to piece together Easterbrooks' interest in the *Wizard of Oz* and the codes that mentioned some of the characters. I couldn't wait to get back to look at those codes again.

I had lunch when I got back to the hotel. Clint came in to tell me I had a visitor. I followed him into the soda fountain. I was surprised to see Grumbera waiting for me—a huge banana split in front of him— probably on the house.

"There you are," he said, when I walked in to get a soda from Clint.

"Yo, Grumbera, what brings you to this heavenly Oasis?"

"*You*," he said.

"Me?"

"Yeah. What have you got?"

"Got?"

"I got this call from Dr. Trexler says you have some info on the case I ought to know about."

My heart started pounding. This was trouble. My mind started chugging to get out of it—like a kid being caught at something he knows he shouldn't be doing and trying to make excuses. "Oh," I said, "I was only trying to get him to hire me. His wife actually. She's bound to be a softer touch, don't you think?"

"Hire you for what?"

"Private detective work. Not easy to live in this town with my police training and no police job. You understand that, don't you, Grumbera?"

"Yeah, I guess," he said. "But what did you tell Mrs. Trexler you had on the case to get her to ask her husband to hire you?"

"Oh, I don't know. I think if I had a little money I might be able to investigate and produce something worthwhile, and," I said, looking at Clint, "might be able to pay my room and board for a couple more weeks."

"I wouldn't be against that," Clint said.

I laughed louder than I would have if I had been alone with Clint. I was trying to take Grumbera's mind from the case. Anything I told him I could kiss goodbye, and my services would be worthless to Dr.

Trexler and possibly Mr. Easterbrook. I had a feeling he wasn't as poor as everyone was leading me to believe. He was in Barbados, for heaven's sakes. Not too many poor people went to Barbados.

"Bones," Grumbera said, "tell me what you got."

"I don't know that I have anything you don't."

"You don't want me to take you in and lock you up, do you?"

"Hmm," I considered the offer. "Three meals a day," I said, "and a bed in a room not much worse than what I got here. Hmm—let me think about it."

"Bones!" Grumbera said.

"Well, I'd be where I belong—with my buddies in the department. Maybe I could put my experience and knowledge to use—I'm not getting much work here as it is." I turned to Clint who was puttering behind the counter, "No fault of yours, Clint," I said.

"Glad to hear it," he said.

"Come on, Bones, I'm taking you in. Let you cool your heels in the lock up and think about sharing."

"Sharing? You share anything with me?"

"That's different," he said.

"Aw now, Grumbera." I said. "We go way back, don't we?"

He nodded.

"I ever do you wrong?"

"No."

"Think I'd try to do you wrong now?"

"Guess not," he admitted. "But it's no matter. I have my orders. You tell me what you got and were trying to sell to Doc Trexler, or I take you in until you remember."

"Grumbera—give me a break. I was bluffing. Making believe I had something so I could get some dough."

"Making believe you had *what?*"

"Gee, Grumbera—look, I'll make you a deal."

"No deals."

"I ever go back on my word with you?"

"Guess not."

"So I'll give you my word. I get anything I think you can use, I'll bring it to you before the FBI."

"Bring it to me first—let me decide if it's worthwhile," he said.

"Fair enough," I said. It seemed to satisfy him. I don't know why. I don't know what 'fair enough' meant to him. I don't even know what it means to me.

I looked at the clock behind the counter. The duchess and the nerd would be here in less than twenty minutes. I thought it would be a lot better to have Grumbera out of the hotel when they came, or he might start asking them questions and I don't think they'd have the smarts not to tell him everything.

But Grumbera showed no sign of going anywhere and with each minute ticking away I became more nervous.

I tried to signal Clint to get rid of Grumbera, but Clint wasn't catching on.

I finally eased my way out of the soda fountain, but nobody seemed to see me go.

Sixteen

I left the hotel and walked down the street in the direction of the school in the hope of meeting the duchess on her way to the hotel so she wouldn't see Grumbera and vice versa. There's no telling what either the duchess or the nerd would tell Grumbera. Whatever they might say was sure to end my part in the case.

I was afraid to walk too far down Broad Street in the direction of the school for fear they would come the other direction and I wouldn't be able to head them off before Grumbera got to them. So I only went as far as I could see in both directions. After five or so minutes I began to wonder if they were coming at all. Perhaps some after-school activity kept them.

No such luck. I saw in the distance two small figures moving toward me, without any particular sense of purpose. I suppose that meant they had not made progress on the codes. I moved rapidly toward them to warn them not to spill the beans to Grumbera.

When I got close enough to be recognized, I said with sunshine in my voice, "Hi, kids, how's it going?"

They both looked at me as though I were a stranger. "It's Bones," I said automatically.

"We know who you are," the duchess said, and I felt a little silly.

They didn't slow down so I fell in step with them.

"Where are Billy and Freddy?" I asked. "Weren't you going to bring them?"

"They don't know anything," the duchess said. "Only that Wanda and Arvilla giggled a lot over some secret."

"Oh," I said.

"Figure anything more out with the codes?" I asked.

"Yeah," the duchess said, without telling me what.

"What did you figure?"

"I'll tell you at the hotel," she said as though reaching her destination were her top priority.

"Oh, well, okay," I said, disappointed. "Oh, by the way," I went on as casually as I could. The last thing I wanted to do was alarm them, because I thought they might react opposite to what I wanted—"Grumbera—the policeman—is at the Broad Street in the soda fountain. I think it best if we keep what we're doing a secret between us. If the police started working on the same thing they would probably mess it up."

Neither kid reacted. "Okay?" I said, trying to get an answer.

"Police, huh?" the nerd asked. "You think they'd be interested in what we're doing?"

"Yeah—but that's the point. I think we should be sure what we have before we go sharing it."

The nerd grunted—the duchess said nothing.

When we got to the hotel lobby I tried to block the entry to the soda fountain to make them go into the dining room. But they both scooted around me as though they'd made up this great football play and couldn't wait to try it out on me.

Clint smiled when he saw them come into the soda fountain shoppe. From his stool at the counter Grumbera smiled at the kids. His banana split was gone. He was a good guy underneath his blue uniform, but that wasn't going to help me out of this pickle.

"Officer," the nerd began, as though he were an adult asking directions in a strange town, "are you working on the case of the two girls..." then he added as an afterthought, "...that disappeared?"

"Sure am," he said. "Was just discussing it with Clint here."

"We're working on it too," he said, and I realized I was doomed.

"Oh yeah," Grumbera said, "what are you doin'?"

"Codes. We found some codes and we're cracking them."

A big, broad grin covered Grumbera's face as he looked down from his stool at the counter on the twelve year-old code crackers. "That's great," he said, putting his hand on the nerd's head and rubbing his hair. "Keep up the good work—someday we'll make a policeman out of you." He looked at the duchess. "You too," he said.

"Okay, kids, Bones," Clint said, "how about some strawberry ice cream today?"

The nerd said, "Yeah, okay." I was frowning. I thought we could have lost it all with that one blunder from the nerd. Now we'd be in clear view of the cop while we slurped our ice cream. We ate in silence for a while, when Grumbera mercifully got up to leave.

"Thanks, Clint," he said. "See you around." He looked over at our table. "Keep up the good work, kids—" then he looked at me with a smile, "—you too, big guy." It had been a long time since I was so relieved to see anyone go out a door like Grumbera did.

"Why did you tell Grumbera about the codes?" I asked the kid. "I told you not to—you're working with me."

"He's a policeman," he explained, "and you're not."

Great, I thought, he has the same prejudice as the adults.

"And that's an advantage for you—with me," I said. "You see how seriously Grumbera took you— you're just kids to him. To me you're both geniuses. He can't work with kids—doesn't know how. I can. Let's go to the dining room. You can show me what you have."

I decided since Calvin was a nerd, he was unpredictable. I rather think he was showing me who was boss with this code thing. He and the duchess were working on it, and I was threatening to go to the cops with it if they didn't meet my deadline. He probably thought the code was his, and if anyone was going to take it to the cops, it was going to be he. I guess I didn't realize my threat could backfire. Fortunately, Grumbera didn't take him seriously.

In the dining room, the backpacks were thrown on the table. Out came the laptop computer, and the sheets of paper with the original codes on them.

I waited for him to volunteer the information he'd found that he tried to tell Grumbera. He didn't. Was I to be snubbed by a twelve year old in addition to everyone else? The funny thing was, I didn't ever remember getting that much respect when I *was* a member of the police department. I decided I had a better relationship with the duchess and I should work through her.

"Duchess," I said, "did you make any progress figuring out what the sentences mean?"

"Yes," she said.

"Did you want to share it with me, or are you only working through official channels? I notice our local officer wasn't too interested in your information."

"You told us if we didn't solve it by today, *you* were going to give it to the experts."

She had me there. "Okay," I said, "you're right. But it looks like our best chance is to work together. So what did you find out?"

"Well," the nerd cut in, "did *you* find anything out?"

Was he trying to rub it in? Was he trying to show me what a hotshot he was with codes? No, I guessed he was just looking for help.

"I've been thinking about X," I said, trying to make it look like I had discovered something important. "We should try to eliminate who it couldn't be. I doubt it is Dr. Trexler—or Mrs. Trexler, or Mrs. Easterbrook. Leonard Yohe is a possibility, but a thin one. I don't really see him having any part of this. I could be wrong. That leaves Mr. Easterbrook—or someone else I haven't thought of. What do you think?"

"I think it's Mr. Easterbrook," the duchess said.

The nerd wasn't sure, but then the duchess pointed out he didn't really know any of the people we mentioned.

"All right," I said, let's just assume it *is* Mr. Easterbrook. How do the other pieces fit?"

"Verity says the thing about the Cowardly Lion could be X's way of saying Arvilla needed the courage to take some chances," the nerd said. "Like running away from home."

"And the Tin Man could be Wanda's father," Verity said, "because she always made it seem like he was cold and didn't have a heart."

"Of course the Tin Man in the *Wizard of Oz* knew he didn't have a heart and he wanted to get one," I said. "Do you think it fits Dr. Trexler?"

"Closer than anyone else we have so far," the duchess said.

"From what Verity tells me, I believe the Tin Man is Wanda's father and the Scarecrow is Arvilla's mother. She wanted a brain," he explained to me, as though I didn't have one myself.

The duchess chimed in. "There was one other

page jammed at the bottom of my bag, which I gave to Calvin."

"Does 'paradise in water' mean anything to you?" the nerd asked me.

"An island in the ocean," I said right away. Maybe the next time they wanted to talk to the cops, they'd listen to me. I was too close to solving it to throw it away on Grumbera. I had two goals: make some money and have the police realize how valuable I was and give me my job back.

Though Wanda and Arvilla never used the name of Arvilla's Dad, I began to believe Mr. Easterbrook was Mr. X. And so many of the coded references were to the land of Oz, I couldn't help but picture the girls on the yellow brick road.

While I was considering the best way to handle the information I now thought we had, the phone rang in the soda fountain and Clint answered it. "It's for you," he said, waving the phone at me.

I went to the counter to take the call.

"Fatzinger," he said with a booming voice, almost scaring me out of my wits.

"Yesss," I said slowly. I never thought it a good sign when someone called me by my last name.

"This is Ken Easterbrook. You wanted me to call you?"

"Oh, yes, thanks." I was surprised. I hadn't really expected him to call me. "I'm working on the case—your daughter and her friend."

"Yes, my secretary told me. Any luck?"

"I think I'm onto something," I said.

"Oh?" he said, and I got the feeling he wasn't

overjoyed. "What have you got?"

"I'd like to talk to you about it," I said.

"I'm listening."

"In person," I dared to say. "Any way you could see me?"

"Well—I'm in Barbados at the moment."

"Coming back any time soon?"

"Oh, no—I'm having a ball. Footloose and fancy free."

"Well—I think it might be worth your while to hear what I have to say."

"Yeah, well, if you can't say it on the phone, maybe it isn't that urgent."

I didn't like what I was hearing, but it did bolster my suspicions.

"Where are you staying?"

"The Princess, but I'm leaving."

"For where?"

"Well, I just go where the money is. No telling in advance."

"Sounds like fun," I said—but I didn't mean it.

"*Is*," he said. "Tell you what, I'll call you tomorrow, see if you can tell me anything then. I'll keep you posted," he said, but somehow I didn't think he would.

Seventeen

What a slippery guy that Easterbrook was. Imagine not knowing where he was going to be tomorrow!

He was so strange on the phone; I was very suspicious.

I made up my mind I had to go to Easterbrook to see for myself if the girls were with him. But how was I going to do that? I didn't know where he was, and he didn't seem about to tell me. Obviously, if he had the girls with him, he wasn't going to admit it.

Also, I didn't have the money to go that far. I didn't even have the money to telephone the area to see if I could track him down.

In the dining room with the kids, the pace of activity seemed to have slowed to the point where they could close shop.

"All finished?" I asked.

"Yup," the nerd said.

"What do you think?" I asked the duchess.

She answered as though she were reading a prepared report. "Mr. X is Mr. Easterbrook. Wanda and Arvilla went with him for a fun trip. They didn't tell their parents because they knew they wouldn't let them go. They went on different days so nobody would suspect they ran away together. Arvilla used to tell me her father wanted her to go on a trip with him."

"Why didn't she?"

"She said she wanted a friend to go along—and he didn't want that."

"You think he changed his mind?"

The duchess shrugged her shoulders. The nerd said, "It looks like it."

"How did they get to Barbados—or wherever they are?"

"We don't know," the duchess said. "Mr. Easterbrook had a girlfriend. Maybe she packed them up and took them to the airport."

"No way," I said. "Two twelve year olds get on a plane unnoticed? I don't think so. Everybody in the country knew two girls were missing."

"Maybe they went to New York City," the nerd said. "It's only ninety miles."

"New York is big, but they'd be picked up right away."

"Maybe the girlfriend went with them," the nerd said.

I shook my head. "The third army could have gone with them and they'd still be stopped. News travels fast these days. Everybody in the country was on the lookout for those girls."

"But together," the nerd asked, "or separate? They went two days apart."

"Yes."

"I've read about private planes," the duchess said. "Maybe they were on a small plane."

"They wouldn't have to go through any security check that way," I agreed. "But private planes are very expensive. I'm not sure Mr. Easterbrook can afford that."

"Can you find out?" the duchess asked.

"I could check everybody around here who charters flights, but maybe Easterbrook had a friend with a plane. Maybe someone in Barbados or Florida or anywhere. It would take years to check them all, and I could still miss."

"Bummer," the nerd said.

"He could be traveling with the two girls with fake identification."

"What identification?" the duchess asked. "They don't have licenses, they're too young to drive. So he tells the airline people Arvilla is his daughter, which she is—and maybe he says Wanda is his stepdaughter."

"She's right," the nerd chimed in. "Kids don't have licenses."

"Ah, but you need a *passport* to get out of the country—and kids can get passports."

"If they got a private plane would they need passports?"

"Probably to get into the country."

"You know what?" the duchess said, as though bells and whistles were going off in her head at a fast pace. "They have passports. Both of them. Wanda's been to Europe with her mom and dad, and Arvilla's been to Barbados before. If they knew where they were going, they would take their passports."

Okay, I did get help from the duchess and the

nerd. But help is not solving the case. I still had miles to go. Oh how I wished I had enough money to just go chasing after them. But dreams like that were burning up precious time.

"What are you going to do next?" the duchess asked me.

"I was just wondering that myself. Any suggestions?"

"You could find out where they are and go after them."

"Exactly," I said. "Good thinking. Only two things stand in the way, and they're both money."

"You need money for a plane ticket?"

"Right."

"What else?"

"To make telephone calls to make sure I don't waste money or airplanes to go on a wild goose chase."

The duchess wrinkled her nose. "A wild goose chase? What's that?"

"Just flying all over the world like a wild goose without knowing where you are going."

"Geese know where they are going," the duchess said. She had an uncanny storehouse of information like that.

"It's just an expression," I said.

"Why don't you ask Dr. Trexler for the money?" the nerd said.

"I already did," I explained. "He went right to the police. Grumbera almost threw me in the slammer."

"Slammer?" the duchess asked.

"Jail," I said. "The place where they slam the

iron doors closed on you."

"You can use the phone here, can't you?" the duchess asked.

"I don't think Clint and Clara would be sympathetic to that, seeing as I am presently somewhat behind on my room and board—"

"Come to my house," the duchess offered.

"You think your mother and father would want me running up a phone bill like that?"

"Why not? When you find the girls you'll get money, won't you?"

"From who?" I asked, giving away my very poor position in the matter. "It won't be Mr. Easterbrook if he has the kids. He's liable to go to jail. Dr. Trexler has already turned me down."

"But, you'll get the reward, won't you?" the duchess asked.

"They have a lot of ways of getting out of paying rewards—so I'm not sure."

"You don't think Dr. Trexler wants Wanda back?" the nerd asked with surprise.

"He wants the police to do it. I guess he doesn't trust me."

"He should trust you *more* than the police," the duchess said. "Why, that Grumbera wouldn't even listen to us when we threw the solution in his lap. I'll talk to him," she said, as though it were the most natural thing in the world.

"Grumbera?" I asked.

"No, Dr. Trexler," the duchess said. "I'll tell him he can trust you."

"Oh, Duchess, that's very nice of you, but I

don't think…I mean, if he wouldn't give me anything, why would he give it to you?'"

"Because he *knows* me. Plus, he likes me."

"But…I'm afraid."

"Of what?"

"He'll get you to tell him everything. He'll take it to the police or the FBI, and I'll be out of a job."

"I won't tell him anything," she said. "He'll trust me. You'll see."

I thought she was dreaming, but I didn't say so. Why should I try to discourage a kid who wanted to help? I certainly got nowhere with Dr. Trexler, and I had no one else to turn to.

"Okay," I said. "If you think you can do it, you're on."

The duchess smiled. "Okay," she said. "Let's go to my house and you can use the phone."

You had to love the kid. It was as though she were paying the phone bill and nothing would be more natural than paying for all the international calls I wanted to make.

We walked the nerd home, and I thanked him for his great help. "If I get the reward," I said feeling particularly generous, "I'll give you and the duchess some of it."

The light in his eyes showed me he liked the idea.

"Of course, you both know if you tell what we are doing to the police or—" I looked at the duchess, "—Dr. Trexler—there won't be a reward for me. Besides," I said, then realized I shouldn't muddy the waters with things the kids probably couldn't understand.

"Besides what?" the duchess pressed.

"Oh, nothing," I said—"it wasn't a good idea."

"No," the nerd said on his doorstep, "besides what?"

"Oh, okay, I was just thinking—Mr. Easterbrook could go to jail for this. He probably thought it was great fun, and I'm sure he has some well-rehearsed explanation, but what he did was kidnapping. I expect he could talk himself out of the kidnapping charge with his daughter—saying he told his wife, but she was so scatterbrained she didn't understand. But explaining Wanda Trexler away will not be as easy. Elsie Trexler is anything but scatterbrained—ditto the doc."

"What will Mr. Easterbrook say about that?" the duchess wanted to know.

"I expect he'll make believe that he thought everyone knew, and he didn't bother to check with the Trexlers."

"But they left without any clothing—without telling anyone," the nerd said, quite reasonably. "How will he explain that?"

"Be tough," I admitted, "but I expect he'll try."

We left him and went on to the duchess's house. Her mother was in the kitchen helping her father make dinner. Ximenes Rafael Manolette Buscador was a trim, regal looking man, with a well defined nose and a straight-as-a-rod posture that any mother would die for.

"Bones!" he said on seeing me, "I have not seen you for a long time—how have you been?"

"I been better," I said. "I been worse."

"Why is that?"

"I'm working on this case," I said, "I find myself in need of making phone calls—but I don't have a phone of my own."

"A telephone?" he said as though that surprised him. "We have a telephone—lots of telephones all over the house. Take your pick—and when you finish, stay for dinner. I'm making my chicken—lots of butter, you'll like it."

"Oh, I don't know if I should," I said, looking at Tad (whose real name was Quintessa).

"Don't look at me," she said, "Xim," as she called him—pronouncing it Heem—"would have the whole world to dinner if they happened to drop by."

"But...how do you feel about it?"

"Oh, don't be so shy, Bones. We know you better than that. Of course if you have a better offer, I'm sure Xim will take a rain check."

I blushed. I didn't have a better offer.

Eighteen

Ximenes was a fabulous cook, and I ate like a horse. He kept offering more, and my ability to refuse was never the best.

Xim—I wondered if there could be the slightest possibility that Xim was X. It certainly would change our thinking. I chose to believe it was just a coincidence. If he had the girls, where would they be? In his basement?

At the dinner table, the duchess said, "Bones needs money to find the girls. So I'm going to talk to Dr. Trexler."

Tad said, "That's very nice of you, Verity, but don't you think Bones should make that request himself?"

"Already did," she said. "Dr. Trexler went to the police."

"Oh dear," Tad said. "But I don't quite see you convincing Dr. Trexler to give Bones the money when Bones couldn't convince him."

"Well, maybe Verity can," Ximenes said. "I'll go with her. It will be a good experience."

"Oh, Xim, she's twelve years old."

Ximenes smiled. "Would it surprise you to learn

I know how old she is? And Dr. Trexler is a lot older. I just think Bones has gotten a bad shake here and maybe we should do something to help him out. Our Verity has been working with him, and it sounds like they've made progress," he said. "Tomorrow is Saturday. We'll go then."

"Oh, Xim," Tad said—"this is not like selling Girl Scout cookies."

"We'll see," he said. "Maybe it'll be easier."

After dinner, I went to the basement to use the telephone to be out of everyone's way, though Tad insisted I wouldn't bother anyone if I used the phone in the kitchen or her office.

In the cozy basement, redone to look like a rustic tavern with tables, a TV, but no bar, I picked up the Mickey Mouse phone and called Barbados information for the Princess Hotel.

I got the number and dialed it. The operator answered.

"Ken Easterbrook, please," I said with a certainty I didn't feel.

"One moment, please." There was a long silence before she came back on the line. "I don't have anyone registered by that name," she said.

"Sure you do," I said, "check again." I spelled it for her, just to be sure.

"One moment, please." Silence. She came back. "No, I'm sorry."

"The gentleman with the two twelve year-old girls," I added, helpfully.

"I wouldn't know about that, I'm just the operator."

"Would you have any information on them if they checked out?"

"I'll check." She came back after a moment. "I don't show them registered at the hotel anytime this month."

"Perhaps he used a fictitious name."

"I wouldn't know that, sir."

"Let me talk to the front desk please."

"One moment, sir."

"Front desk," a man's voice came on the line.

"Yes," I said. "A gentleman just called me from your hotel—his name is Ken Easterbrook—the operator has no record of him—I wondered if you might."

"One moment, sir." They were all good at saying that.

He came back. "I'm sorry, sir, I don't show any Easterbrooks registered at this hotel.

"But surely you remember him. He's the American with the two twelve year-old girls."

"Isn't ringing any bells with me. Are you sure you have the right hotel?"

"This the Princess?"

"Yes it is."

I called back and asked for the dining room. A man answered. "I'm looking for Ken Easterbrook," I said. "The guy with the two twelve year olds. Is he eating there by any chance?"

"I don't see anyone like that here now," he said.

"Anyone like that before this week?"

"No, sir, not that I can recall."

I had visions of this guy being on the receiving

end of a big tip from Easterbrook to keep quiet—but what if everyone got tips to lie? But, speaking of lying, it was starting to look like Easterbrook was lying to me when he said he was at the Princess. It would make sense, if he kidnapped the kids, to lie about where he was.

But how did he plan to explain what he was doing? If the kids were with him, they were not restrained. Kidnapping across state lines was punishable by death. That's why you hardly hear of it anymore. But, if he said he was in Barbados at the Princess, and no one saw them—I expect he really *was* there alone.

I made one more call to the hotel to housekeeping. A woman answered but was no help. I told her I left my watch in my room.

"What room, sir?"

"I'm embarrassed to say I can't remember the number. I was the guy with the two girls—twelve year olds—my daughter and her friend."

"I'd have to have the room number, sir. Check with reception, they'll tell you."

"Surely you remember the room with the two twelve year-old girls."

"We have a lot of rooms, sir. There have been many children here. I'm sorry I can't help you."

"So did you find my watch in *any* room?"

"No watch was turned in here."

"Thanks."

I was afraid my lack of success in locating Easterbrook and the girls was not a good sign for collecting money to go to Barbados. If I didn't have more evidence they were there, it would only be one of those wild goose chases. Not only wouldn't Trexler give me the money—a long shot in any case—but I wouldn't take the trip. I wasn't interested in any vacation of my own.

I went upstairs to where the Buscadors were seated in the living room.

I shook my head. "Either Easterbrook was lying about being at the Princess in Barbados, or everyone there is doing a fantastic job of covering it up."

"Sit down," Ximenes offered. "What are you going to do?"

The duchess seemed to be in another world, twisting her hands.

"I don't know," I said. "On the one hand, if Easterbrook is lying to me, that makes me suspicious. But he could have been calling from Tamaqua, Pennsylvania for all I know. This Princess Hotel could have just been to throw me off."

Out of the blue, the duchess said, "Maybe it's the Princess, but not the hotel."

What kind of idea was that, I wondered. Sometimes I got a funny feeling about twelve year-old wisdom.

"Are you talking about the movie, *The Princess Bride?* Maybe he took them to that movie—if it's playing again anywhere."

"Could be a video," Ximenes offered.

"Up in their room at the Princess Hotel?" I asked.

"Isn't there a Princess Hotel in Acapulco, Mexico?" Tad asked. "And Bermuda?"

"All over," I said. "Probably in Africa, Vegas, and Atlantic City for all I know. But the code said a watery paradise—I'm thinking that has to be an island."

There was a silence while I could almost hear everyone thinking.

"Maybe it's not an island," the duchess broke the silence.

"No? What kind of watery paradise is not an island? The seashore?"

"No," the duchess said, and then she seemed to pause for effect. It drove me crazy. Then she announced as though she had discovered America—"A ship—there's a Princess ship."

Ximenes clapped his hands—"That could be it. Verity, that's brilliant."

Well, I didn't think it was that brilliant. Of course, I knew there were Princess ships, but where they were was another matter—and if Easterbrook was on one, and if the girls were with him, was another matter entirely. But I didn't say anything because I didn't want to step on the duchess's big moment. I believed in encouraging kids just as much as Ximenes did, even if they were far off the mark, which I feared she was in this instance.

"Well, I guess if they are all on a cruise there isn't much danger. Maybe the thing is a big misunder-standing."

"I know a couple of parents who would be very surprised to hear that," Tad said. "Why don't we ask Irene if there's a Princess ship around Barbados."

"Who's Irene?" I asked.

"She's a travel agent and a friend of mine," Tad said. "Lives just down the street. I'll call her."

Tad went to the kitchen to use the phone. The duchess sat with that maddening expression on her face. The one that said, I know I'm right. I wasn't so sure about that. For a ship to be in Barbados on this exact date was a long shot at best. But I held my tongue as I always did when the duchess had one of her strange brainstorms. The funny thing was Ximenes was smiling too, as though he already knew the answer.

We heard the muffled telephone conversation in the kitchen, but we couldn't hear the words. My mind was on what my next move would be after we found out the Princess ships were all in Alaska or the Mediterranean Sea or somewhere far away from Barbados.

It seemed like one hundred years before Tad came back to the living room with the news. It was probably only five minutes or so.

"Irene says the Caribbean Princess was in Barbados yesterday and today, and is sailing to other Caribbean ports for another week."

Ximenes clapped his hands again. "That's my Verity," he said, "she's a *genius*. Didn't I tell you?"

So what was I, I wondered—chopped liver?

Nineteen

Irene brought the Princess Cruises brochure to the Buscador's door, proving she was not only a good neighbor and friend, but a driven travel agent as well.

I opened to the Caribbean cruises and there in black and white was the trip they were surely on. It had left a few days after the girls were missing and still had about five days more to run.

I asked Irene if we could verify passengers with the cruise line. She promised to see what she could do. Ordinarily they didn't give out that information, but she had a contact who might be able to tell her something.

Ximenes and the duchess were scheduled to see Dr. Trexler in the morning, in an attempt to succeed where I had not. I didn't hold much hope for them, but no stone unturned was my philosophy.

I thanked the Buscadors for the dinner and bid them goodbye.

Ximenes said they would see me tomorrow "with, I hope, good news."

He was such a cheerful, optimistic guy.

My realistic streak caused me to compare getting money from Dr. Trexler to getting honey from lemons.

The hotel soda fountain was jumping when I got back. That was the downside of living there. Friday and Saturday night could get a little noisy.

When I walked in the front door I heard a familiar voice hail me from the counter. "Bones! Ol' buddy, come in here and let me buy you an ice cream soda."

I looked in the room and saw Grumbera with his big belly touching the counter. He was out of uniform—off duty.

I was plenty tired, but I was afraid to refuse. Grumbera could always put me in jail for not sharing what I had—but I also knew he was going to pump me for information that I didn't want to give him.

"Hi, Grumbera," I said without going in the room—"thanks for the offer, but I'd like a raincheck if I could—I'm pretty tired."

"Tired? From what? Who cares—you can sleep all day tomorrow—it's Saturday—come to think of it you can sleep all day any day—you're not working."

For some reason the kids in the soda fountain thought that was funny. I didn't share their amusement. Grumbera kept waving me in, I decided I'd better go—just for a minute.

"What're you having?" Grumbera said.

"I'll have a birch beer on tap."

"Well, holy smokes—Clint—draw a birch for the big man—don't worry about getting paid—I'm paying."

Clint drew the birch and handed it over the counter to me. "Your health," he said. Clint was a jovial fellow. You had to like him.

"Well, Bones," Grumbera said, "how the heck are you?"

"Fine," I said, "real good. Yourself?"

"Great, Bones, just great," Grumbera said. "I'm always great when I'm off duty."

We all chuckled.

"I guess you must be super-great," he said, "since you're off duty all the time."

I don't know why these kids thought that was so funny. I could see what kind of night this was going to be—Grumbera was going to get his kicks needling me.

"So tell me, Bones," he said in a half-whisper that carried throughout the room—"what have you got on the missing girls case? Just between us buddies."

"Yeah," I said, "buddies. I don't think I have anything that would interest you or any other professional lawman. I'm just horsing around, keeping my hand in the game. You can imagine how tough that is without the resources and backing of a real police department."

Some big kid down the counter said, "Real police department? Where's that? Not in Ephesus."

A roar of approval went up, and I noticed it was a laugh that didn't please Grumbera.

"No," Grumbera said, "no kidding." His voice was lower now that he realized the jokes could be turned on him. "Clint says you have these kids here working on codes. Is there anything to that?"

"Oh, you know kids. I've become sort of friendly with the duchess—you know, Verity Buscador—Tad's kid. She doesn't have a lot of friends and she comes here everyday. The codes are like a game with us. Gives us both something to pass the time—like playing solitaire," I said, needling Grumbera a little for all the time he spent playing solitaire on the department computer.

"Well, we have a deal, don't we?" Grumbera said, staring sadly ahead at the mirror behind what used to be the bar.

"Don't we have a deal?" Grumbera prodded, since I hadn't answered him.

"What deal?" I asked.

"You told me if you had anything good on the case you'd share it with me. I didn't put you in jail based on that promise."

"Oh, yeah," I said, "right."

"That's still good, is it?"

"Sure."

"And you swear this code business is nothing I'd want?"

"Hey, Grumbera, what are you talking about? The kid wanted to talk codes with you and you turned him off."

"Yeah," he said, "maybe I made a mistake. Maybe I should see what he has. What was his name?"

"I don't know. I just called him Nerd."

"Well, put me in touch with him, will you?"

"Sure, Grumbera," I said, "I mean, if you don't mind the ribbing you'd take, turning to a twelve year-old nerd to solve your cases."

I got my laugh.

"Yeah, well," Grumbera said, blushing, "if you won't tell me what you got—and heck, I don't blame you—all the years you put in the force here in Ephesus, they could have treated you better."

"Thanks, Grumbera."

"So you mouthed off a little about the mayor and the chief—how stupid they were. But the thing was a lousy ten-buck robbery, how could you know how seriously they'd take you paying the poor sucker's grocery bill? And how could you have known the mayor was in the next room listening?"

"Yeah," I said, "thanks, Grumbera."

"Chain of command is very important to Pennsylvania Germans—insubordination is like armed robbery. Of course, you were pretty colorful in your descriptions of the mayor pushing the chief to solve it, and the chief being all thumbs." Grumbera was giving me the benefit of the doubt, which was something nobody did around these parts. "I mean, nobody's perfect."

"Well, Grumbera, buddy, I got to hit the hay."

"Big day tomorrow?"

"All my days are little ones—but I still like to be awake for them."

"Okay, buddy—our deal is still on then?"

"Oh, yeah," I said, "and thanks for the drink."

He saluted me as I left. I decided that would have been a nice goodbye—unless he was making fun of me.

I was at a late breakfast the next morning when the duchess and her dad came into the dining room. Ximenes was smiling—the duchess had her typical blank stare, but her mouth was drawn into a wide, nervous smile so uncharacteristic it seemed rehearsed.

"Good news," she said. "Dr. Trexler gave me the money."

At first I couldn't believe my ears. I thought she was trying to say something else, and it didn't come out right. "The money?" I said, catching on. "He *did?* That's great, Verity! How much?"

"Two thousand."

"Two thousand?" I looked at her dad for his confirmation. He smiled broadly and nodded. "My Verity did it," he said. "I was so proud of her. She asked for the money like a grownup—hinted that if he loved his daughter, he couldn't refuse. He was on the spot. He tried to pump her for what you knew, but she didn't tell him! She said that would compromise your investigation. Oh, baby, I was just *so* proud of you."

"Good work, Duchess," I said. "May I have the check?"

The duchess frowned. Uh oh, I thought, there *is* no check. Just a promise that could easily be forgotten.

When the duchess didn't answer—or make any move to produce the check, her father said, "It's all right, Verity, show him the check."

Verity looked at her father. "You tell him," she said.

"That's okay," Ximenes said. "You can tell him."

"Tell me what?"

"Dr. Trexler didn't make the check to you."

"He didn't?"

"No. He said he'd only make it to me, because I was so convincing."

"Oh," I said, taking the insult as well as could be expected—which wasn't that well at all.

"It's okay," Ximenes said. "We go to the bank now—it's open till noon. Verity will endorse the check to you. Irene is already looking into the best way for you to go to the Caribbean and intercept the ship."

Well, the whole thing knocked me out. I put my arm around the duchess and gave her a hug. "That's good work, Duchess," I said.

The three of us went over to the bank, and when I saw how important it made my twelve year-old buddy feel to sign that check over to me, I realized the whole thing was worth it.

Buddy? Perhaps I should call her partner.

When our business was completed and I put the money in my starving checking account, I realized it was more money than I'd had in my account since I'd been booted off the force.

I smiled again at the duchess and gave her an even bigger hug than before. "Good job, Duchess, a real good job!"

"Thank you," she said, dropping her head shyly.

"Irene is waiting for you," Ximenes said. "She's working at home since it's Saturday. You get your tickets, and a visitor pass for the ship, then you come to our place for lunch."

"Sounds good to me," I said, and we were off to Irene, the travel agent.

Twenty

I packed lightly for my flight to the Caribbean Island of St. Stephen. I wasn't expecting to stay long.

Irene had booked my flights, and Ximenes insisted on driving me to the airport with the duchess. She wanted to go along to the island in the worst way, but her father and I agreed it would not be right. So she sulked all the way to the airport, saying things like—"I got you the money. I got you the code. I got you the translation. Why *can't* I go?"

I was to land at St. Stephen in the evening before the ship docked. Irene got me a hotel room near the dock, and I was all set.

She was able to get minimal information from her contact in the Princess Cruises accounting department. She verified Easterbrook had paid with his credit card, but she couldn't, or wouldn't say who (if anyone) was on the ship. It was the management's protection of the passenger's privacy.

The duchess wasn't a happy camper when I boarded the plane. "I promise I'll call you first after we have the girls safe," I told her. The ship was going to be in port until two PM that next afternoon, so I'd have about six hours to make everything work. That was *after* I verified the girls were on the ship with Easterbrook.

The flight was smooth and landed on time. I took a taxi to the hotel. The driver was a tall, dark-skinned man with a gold chain around his neck, and a white shirt that opened to the top of his black pants. He told me to call him Zack. I questioned him about the ships that docked on the island.

"Oh, is good business. Very busy when ships come. Tomorrow is ship."

"Where do people go here?"

"Oh, they go out to the big hotel, they go to beaches—sightsee the island. We have artist studio, snorkel. They is many things to do."

"How long do they stay on the island?"

"Some only an hour, some come off in the morning and back on the ship by lunch."

"Are there organized tours?"

"Yes. Many buses."

"All those buses hurt the taxi business?" I asked.

"Is okay," he said. "I make living. I want more work I can drive taxi in New York."

"These bus tours—how long do they last?"

"Some three hours—some five hours."

"How much can you make on a good day with a ship in port?"

He mentioned an amount, modest by our US standards. "Would you work for me all day for another ten?"

"Whew—yes, *sir*."

"Good," I said. "How close to the ship can you park?"

"I can pull right up to the dock—but I can't go

on the dock unless I'm delivering a fare."

"Can we see people getting off the ship from where you can park?"

"Yes—through a chain link fence."

My visitor pass said that between 10 a.m. and 1 p.m. I could get aboard. I expected Easterbrook and his guests would be long gone by then, and I didn't want to miss them.

"Can you show me the dock?"

"I can, sure enough. Not far from your hotel."

We drove down the street and turned off to a road that serviced the port.

"Where does the Princess anchor, Zack?" I asked.

"Depends on weather, and if there's room on the exact day," he said. "Sometimes at the dock, sometimes they anchor and bring the passengers in on life boats."

"So we can park here—without being bothered? No police or port people will chase us away?"

"We can park. But, if too many are ahead of us in line, we might not have a good view."

"How early would you have to come to be in a position to see?"

"'Bout six," he said.

"Can you do it?"

"Sure. You still want me to pick you up?"

"Why don't I just walk over. How far to the hotel?"

"It's right there," he said, smiling and pointing to a tropical looking building across the main road.

So the deal was made. I paid the fare from the

airport, and he offered to help me into the hotel, but I said I could manage my small bag myself.

Overhead fans in the hotel tried to cool the hot, humid air. My room was simple and comfortable. The window looked out through palm trees to the water.

I had a good dinner of fish cooked with coconut and bananas. I went to my room and took the cell phone Tad had loaned me, then I called the Ephesus police.

Milton Urfer answered the phone. "Hi, Milt," I said. "It's Bones. Grumbera there?"

"He's off," he said. "Help you?"

"Just looking for him—I'll try him at home."

"Okay," he said. "Or maybe the Broad Street. I think he might have been heading that way."

I called the Broad Street. Clint answered. "Hi, Clint, it's Bones."

"Bones—how you been?"

"Is Grumbera there?"

"Sure is," he said—"I'll put him on."

In a moment, Grumbera took the phone—"Yo, Bones, what's happening?"

"Remember our deal?"

"Yeah."

"I may have something."

"What is it?"

"Not in a position to say for certain. Where will you be tomorrow?"

"Where will I be? Well, holy smokes, Bones, I'll probably be sunning my legs in Atlantic City. Maybe taking in a Broadway show or flying to the moon—

whatever strikes my fancy. How about you?"

"No jokes, Grumbera. When will you be in the office? I may need you."

"*Need* me—that's a new one. You aren't in any kind of trouble, are you, Bones?"

"No, no…"

"Eight to four is my shift tomorrow. Barring any unforeseen stealing of the drugstore's petty cash, I should be there. Why?"

"Tell you tomorrow."

"Hey, why are you calling me—you *live* here for crying outloud," he said. "Where are you, Bones?"

"Gotta run," I said. "Talk to you tomorrow."

"Bones?"

I hung up and began to imagine Grumbera stewing at the Broad Street about my mystery call.

Under the excited circumstances, I guess I had a pretty good night's sleep. I woke at dawn and panicked when I looked out the window and saw the ship was already in the waters offshore. I threw on my clothes and ran down to the dock, pausing just long enough to grab my Polaroid camera and Tad's cell phone.

I ran all the way to the dock, but I needn't have bothered—the ship was there, but no one had gotten off.

I found Zack third in line and I got in the front seat with him. He waved off the glares of the two cabbies in front.

"You're early," he said.

"I saw the ship and got afraid I missed them."

"Nobody off yet. Our authorities have to board

and clear the ship—makes work for our people. Word is there won't be anybody off until eight. Why don't you go back and have some breakfast. You have a couple hours."

I took his advice and went back to the hotel dining room, where I sat under the ceiling fans near a wall open to the outside to let the heat and humidity in—even at this early hour.

I asked the waiter, who brought me my orange juice and tropical fruit—mangos, papaya, pineapple and some berries—where the local police station was.

He smiled. "Just down the street. This is a small place. Everything is just down the street."

I finished my leisurely breakfast and suddenly realized I had left the room in such a hurry, I'd forgotten my binoculars. I went to the room to get them, then returned to Zack in his cab by the dock.

We made small talk for another half hour until I saw the crew preparing the small boats to bring in the passengers. I watched through my binoculars. There was a lot of preparation from the crew before the first boat was loaded. Unfortunately we were positioned so we couldn't see the people getting on the lifeboats—but when they came ashore I'd have a shot at them—if brief. If they were getting on one of the fifteen or so waiting buses I'd have only a short time— as long as it took them to walk from the dock to the bus, a distance of not much more than a basketball court.

"Any way I can get closer?" I asked Zack.

"You can't get inside the gate," he said. "We can move up as soon as someone takes those two cabs ahead of us. You have a pretty clear view here—and if he has two girls with him, he should be easy to spot."

The first boatload docked, and two crew members stood on either side of the exit and helped the passengers out. They hurried to the buses—some just walked out of the gate to tour on their own. A few took cabs—we moved to first place and Zack told the drivers behind him he already had the fare and they could get the next ones.

"Unless my man comes for a cab," I said. "Then we take him."

"What *you* gonna do?"

"Ride in front with you—a friend—a native—a local doctor on a mission of mercy. Anything you want. But I don't think we're going to be that lucky.

"Don't know," he said. "If there are three of them, a cab is lot less money than the bus. I hear the ship bus fares are out of sight."

Lifeboat after lifeboat docked and passengers streamed ashore—but I saw no sign of Easterbrook or the girls. I was beginning to think I'd gotten something seriously wrong. Perhaps they got off for good at the last stop—or maybe they decided to stay on the ship. My hope was the girls overslept and would appear at any moment. They didn't. Was I going to be embarrassed with all the people who had put their faith in me—even gave me money? It looked as if I was going to come up empty handed.

Then it happened. Like a lightning bolt, I saw them get off the lifeboat. The two girls I spotted right away—kids trying to look grown up—cute but self-conscious, taking in the sights, but pretending it was nothing special to smart girls like them. They were wearing t-shirts with the ship's logo on them. Their leader, Ken Easterbrook, was tall and handsome. He reminded me of a few movie stars. He walked through this strange country as though he belonged here.

There was one bus left, but they walked past it for the gate.

"Tell the guys you want this one—get the girls in here. Tell them they won a free fare—anything. Then let me off somewhere and pick me up later. Where can you take them? Is there some sight that'll take ten to fifteen minutes so I can make a call?"

"I'll handle it."

"Then come back for me—that's how they get a free fare. You just love Americans or I'm paying or something. Maybe an American saved your life."

The trio was coming out of the gate—Zack approached Easterbrook and shook his head and pointed to the cab and said something, probably about me and his love for Americans. I wasn't optimistic Easterbrook would swallow it, but I underestimated his eye for a bargain.

My heart leaped up as they came toward the cab. I slumped down in the seat and pulled my cap down over my eyes.

Zack opened the back door for three people who looked better to me than any three people I'd ever seen.

"Too hot to walk," Zack was saying as they piled in.

"Wake up, Jack," he said—"we have company."

I made some noises, stirred my big body a little

and said a sleepy, "Yeah."

Zack started the car. "I'll show you all the sights," he said—like I said, "less than a bus ticket. Having a good time, girls?"

"Uh huh."

"*Are* they?" Easterbrook said. "They're having the time of their lives. They stay up until all hours, then they can't get up in the morning. I was afraid we'd miss the boat."

I didn't stir.

"Are we in Oz or what, girls?" Easterbrook asked.

"Yeah," Wanda said.

"Follow the yellow brick road," Easterbrook said.

"Artist Studio," Zack said. "We'll stop and you can see it. We have a lot of artists here. Oh, this is the—police station," he said half-turned to his passengers in back.

"Got to behave, girls," Easterbrook said, "or you'll wind up in there."

The girls giggled.

I checked it out. So when Zack stopped the car at the artist's studio, I got out and took my cell phone.

"Look out for the Wicked Witch of the West," Easterbrook said.

"Cool," Wanda said.

I went toward the police station and when I was out of sight, I dialed Grumbera in Ephesus. Did I have news for him.

Twenty-one

"Officer Peters," he said.

"Grumbera, it's Bones."

"Yes, Bones—this better be good."

"Is."

"Because we're getting tired of your tricks."

"No trick," I said. "I found them."

"You what?"

"Here's what I want to do. I want you to get credit for the arrest—all I want is the reward."

"Well, I don't control that."

"Maybe not, but what you say will go a long way."

"Slow down, Bones, where are you?"

"The reward, Grumbera—do I qualify for the reward?"

"Well, if you found them, I don't see why not."

"No tricks about me not being eligible because I'm an *ex*-cop?"

"I hope not."

"Well, why don't you find out? I'll call you back. There is not a lot of time—I'm going to call you in five minutes. No reward for me, kiss them good-bye!"

"Bones! What are you talking about?"

"The reward, Grumbera. Talk to the powers that be. I can deliver on a silver platter. You make all the arrangements with the cops here."

"Where? The cops where?"

"Get me the reward, then we'll talk."

"Hey, I can't get you the reward before you deliver."

"All I need is your word, Grumbera. I'll trust you."

"I give you my word, I'll do my best."

"Not good enough. Get the chief—the mayor, whoever to say they'll give it to me if I produce the kids," I said. "Their bad opinion of me is no secret. But, I can make the department look good. Up to the powers that be."

"Hey—you didn't kidnap them?"

"No—I'll prove that—I'll call in five minutes—last chance," and I hung up. I looked at my watch, then down the street. I didn't know how long Zack could stall them.

To help kill the five minutes, which moved painfully slow, I called the duchess, as promised. She answered the phone as she almost never did. I should have realized she would be sitting by, eager for news.

"Duchess," I said, "I found them."

"Good!" she said.

"But we still have to arrange to get them back safely—so don't tell anyone yet. It could spoil it."

"I won't."

"I gotta run. I just wanted you to know right away. I'll tell you more later. Goodbye."

"Goodbye," she said.

I looked down the street. Zack was doing a good job of stalling the Wizard of Oz and his Munchkins—I called Grumbera back.

"Peters," he said, short and gruff.

"Grumbera—Bones."

"Yeah, okay—you're on. Let's have the details."

"I'm on? What are the guarantees?"

"I talked to the mayor. He's head of the reward committee. He says you found them, you get the reward."

"Thanks, Grumbera, I appreciate it. I did record it so there won't be any misunderstanding."

There was silence on his end.

"That's okay, isn't it?" I asked.

"Don't trust me, Bones?" He didn't sound pleased.

"Trust your brother, but cut the cards."

"Okay, we're wasting time. What's the scoop?"

"I'm walking to the police station now. I'm going to tell them the story, then you tell them to arrest and extradite them—or make a deputy out of me and I'll bring them back. You meet the plane and take over."

"Have to talk to the chief. How can I reach you?"

I gave him Tad's cell phone number. "But arrange it with the cops here. I think we need their help to get them on the plane. Maybe a local cop will come along. You'd have to advance money, of course, and he might compete with you for the attention."

I'd made it to the police station. Their operation looked smaller than ours. A lone officer in brown pants and white shirt was sitting behind a desk, an open newspaper set out in front of him on the desk. He looked up at me briefly, then back at the paper as though he'd decided in that glance I was neither a threat nor in distress.

"Morning," I said.

"Morning," he said. "What can I do for you?"

"I have a kidnapper. I need help arresting him."

"Kidnapper?" he asked skeptically. "What he kidnap?"

"Two twelve year-old girls."

His interest was at last engaged.

"Where is he?"

"Down the street."

"How'd he get here?"

"Cruise ship."

The policeman smoothed his white shirt as though he had to look his best for the crowd. "Well," he said, "I can't just lock him up on your say so. I don't even know who you are."

"I'm Bones Fatzinger, private detective—from Ephesus, Pennsylvania."

"Ephesus? What kind of name is that?"

"It's biblical. I want to put you in touch with the Ephesus police—Pete Peters is the officer's name. Why don't you call information—verify the number of the Ephesus cops, and call him. He'll tell you what I'm saying is true and you can work out with him how to get them back."

The man looked dumbfounded, but I saw him pick up the phone and ask for information.

I took his number and told him I'd contact him

at my next opportunity—then I went back down the street to meet Zack with his passengers who were coming out of the artist's studio as a busload of people were coming in.

"Like that, girls?" Zack asked his passengers as I crawled in the front seat.

"It was okay," Arvilla said without enthusiasm.

Fortunately the only one of the three I'd ever seen was Arvilla, and she was certainly not expecting to see anyone from Ephesus on St. Stephen Island. She was also so self-absorbed that with my hat pulled down I was getting away with it.

"You like ocean cruising?" I asked the girls.

"Yeah," Arvilla said.

"Fun," Wanda added.

I let it go at that. They weren't very communicative, but I had second thoughts about cutting short their trip. I even thought about letting them finish the cruise, *then* arresting them, but that seemed like it might be taking too much of a chance. Maybe from there Easterbrook wanted to do Europe with them.

We stopped at a luxury hotel. It was hot and humid and the girls wanted a drink. Zack took them in while I hid out of sight and called the local cops.

The cop had reached Grumbera and was satisfied. I could take them back—he would put them on the plane with me, and Grumbera would meet us when we landed in New York. I told him where the Wizard was so he could make the arrest.

Then I called Dr. Trexler. He answered the phone.

"Doctor," I said, "this is Bones Fatzinger, I've found your daughter," and I paused, I don't know why I wanted to make the Tin Man suffer. If he truly didn't have a heart it would have been no use.

"Is she all right?" he asked anxiously.

"Yes," I said, "she's all right. I'm bringing her back," I said. "It shouldn't take more than a day or so. I'll let you know."

"Wait," he said, "shouldn't the police be doing this?"

"I'm working with the police," I said. "The important thing is you're getting your daughter back, and she's unharmed."

I couldn't resist giving him that small lecture.

Zack was standing by the dining room, keeping an eye on our "guests," while they had sodas. Dad may have been having something stronger—one of those drinks with the little paper umbrellas in them.

"All set?" he asked.

"All set," I said. "They should be coming here. We'll take them to the airport."

"What will happen to the father?"

"He's only the father of one. The other is her friend, Wanda. No one took the trouble to tell her parents she was going. He will probably say he thought Wanda told them."

The police came just as the waiter was bringing the check to the table. Zack and I moved in so we could hear what was being said.

"What are you talking about?" Easterbrook asked, not happy with the turn of events.

"You're under arrest, sir."

"For what?"

"Kidnapping."

"Kidnapping? That's ridiculous. This is my own daughter and her friend. We're on a cruise. Call the captain—he has charge of this ship. You can't…"

"On the ship, sir. But you're on our land now. I have orders to arrest you and put you on a plane with this gentleman here."

Wizard Easterbrook looked at me and squinted. "I thought you looked familiar. You were that cop they threw off the force—what are you doing here?"

"Long story," I said, "I'll tell you on the plane."

"But…b—what *is* this? It's a nightmare is what it is—this is perfectly innocent—why am I being arrested?"

"The Trexlers don't think it's so innocent," I said. "They were worried to death. Can you blame them?"

"But, Wanda, didn't you *tell* them?"

Wanda looked embarrassed. "They wouldn't have let me come," she said.

I didn't argue. We'd have time on the plane for him to try to sell me on his defense.

At the airport, the policeman and Zack stayed with us for the three hours until the plane came.

"I want to call my lawyer," Easterbrook said.

"Plenty of time for that when you get back to your country," the policeman said.

I excused myself and went outside the airport and called the duchess.

She answered on the first ring.

"We have them," I said. "I'm at the airport

waiting for a plane to bring them back."

I couldn't hear anything from the duchess, but I could see her smile in my mind.

Ximenes, her father, got on the phone and was overjoyed at the news. "I'll bring Verity to the airport," he said.

We finally got on the plane, and by now the seriousness of the situation was sinking deep into the Wizard of Oz, and he was starting to perspire. "They don't seriously think I kidnapped my daughter and her friend?"

"I'm afraid I think they seriously do," I said. "And I am having trouble thinking you are surprised—since I told you about it on the phone and it did not seem surprising to you then. In fact, you let me believe you didn't know where the girls were, and they were with you all the time."

"I didn't want to spoil it for them," he said.

The Munchkins were quiet in front of us. They were letting the Wizard make the defense.

I asked Easterbrook how he managed to get the girls out without notice.

"I have a girlfriend," he said, "well, forget that. I don't want anybody else to get in trouble. It was a fun thing. An adventure. Sure, we could have gone the usual route, but it wouldn't have been much fun. Besides, Arvilla and Wanda both said the Trexlers were too uptight to let Wanda go."

"Couldn't you have sent a note or something to tell everyone the girls were okay—and would be back in a week or so?"

"I thought about it. I guess I didn't think

there'd be such a fuss. Arvilla was supposed to tell her mother to tell the Trexlers."

"Arvilla," I said over the seat, "did you?"

She gave a little sound like a puppy coughing. "I forgot," she said.

"How did the girls get to Florida?"

"Got a buddy with a small plane of his own. Owed me a favor. Took off from New Jersey someplace—Wanda spent two nights with my friend, then Arvilla joined her and they drove to Trenton."

"But surely you know it looked like someone kidnapped the girls?"

"I guess analyzing stuff in advance is not my strong point."

I guess that was an understatement. Well, not my business now. In a little while he could tell his story to the police. Grumbera would be a big shot.

When we landed and got off the plane, it was quite a homecoming.

Grumbera was there and put handcuffs on Mr. Easterbrook, who continued to protest his innocence. I had mixed feelings. I think I needed him to be guilty so I could qualify for the reward. On the other hand, I liked the idea of the lark—the surprise trip—though I couldn't agree to making Wanda's parents suffer like that. No one deserved that, no matter how cold they were to their children.

Grumbera let Easterbrook call his lawyer in the airport. He promised to meet him at the Ephesus lockup.

But the big news was that Wanda and Arvilla were so glad to see the duchess waiting for them at the airport—they gurgled and cooed over her—a familiar face their age in the middle of all the strange excitement that surrounded their cut-short vacation.

Maybe the duchess would have real friends out of the deal.

Well, we got home all right—and, you can imagine, I didn't get my reward. Not all of it.

Easterbrook pled guilty to some lesser charge, and he was let off with 1,000 hours of community service and the promise not to do it again.

The Trexlers were so happy to have Wanda back (happier than she was, apparently) that they didn't have the heart to prosecute Easterbrook. Without the surprise disappearance, the trip would have been a fun idea.

As for Wanda and Arvilla, their parents talked to each other and decided on grounding for six months. I guess at twelve, six months seems like forever. Then, after six months, they were made to work at the local senior citizen center—reading books to blind people, changing bed sheets, and washing dishes. They went every weekend for a year—and not together: Arvilla on Saturday; Wanda on Sunday, then they switched. They could only get off with a doctor's excuse that they were sick. Dr. Trexler was in charge of the excuses and he couldn't be fooled. Arvilla tried twice for a school basketball game and a dance, but he wasn't fooled.

Maybe the experience gave the Tin Man, Dr. Trexler, a heart after all. He said we didn't have to pay back the 2,000 dollars he gave the duchess and he gave me another 2,000 dollars "for my trouble." After that, I referred to Wanda Trexler as the 4,000 dollar kid.

The reward committee argued and argued. They finally determined it wasn't a *real* kidnapping after all, and since the Trexlers were not pressing charges and Easterbrook would not go to jail, some reduction in the reward was called for. They gave me forty percent, or 10,000 dollars. Better than a kick in the pants, and enough to pay my debt to Clint and Clara at the Broad Street, and to pay some months in advance, and to repair my car and have a little left over to see me through to my next case.

The duchess put it best. "Let's do this again," she said after we got back from Oz.

Here are the codes that are in the book if you want to try to decode them. The answers appear at the bottom of page 153. No peeking!!

8 X pz ylhkf.

_____

6 X xfdx lt.

_____

3 X ucau lcmg.

_____

10 Fxwc wnnm cx cjtn jwhcqrwp?

_____

Ƨ Swjp pk ck pk kv?

_____

Ɫ Lygygvyl nby fcih.

_____

4 wkh wlq pdq zloo iuhdn.

_____

5 csy lezi e xmr qer, m lezi e wgevigvsa.

_____

Ɛ nypybgqc gl uyrcp.

_____

Tvg zdzb uiln gsv drxpvw drgxs lu gsv dvhg.

_____

22 D xvio rvdo ajm ocz tzggjr wmdxf mjvy.

_____

X is ready.
X says go.
X says Jake.
Won't need to take anything?
Want to go to Oz?
Remember the Lion.
The Tin Man will freak.
You have a Tin Man, I have a Scarecrow.
Paradise in water.
Get away from the Wicked Witch of the West.
I can't wait for the yellow brick road.